FLY ME

Shirley Ann Wilder

"Wilder is the queen of quirky humor, fast-paced drama and heartwarming characters—the perfect combination for a must-read book."

—EmKay Connor, Golden Heart finalist, author of *Willing to Learn*

ON THIN ICE

"What's the matter?" Flip had no idea what he'd done to bring on her rage, which resembled a deep-freeze set on fire.

"The matter is you. You arrogant, meddling, lying, overblown, conceited jet jockey. 'Best if nothing out of the ordinary shows up in her file?' Just whose record were you really protecting?" Ronnie nailed him to the door, jabbing her finger into his chest, her words slicing through him like a blade through a ripe watermelon.

When Ronnie whirled away, Flip took the advantage and moved to the center of the room, giving her a wide berth as she grabbed her jacket and handbag from the chair.

She started for the door, then spun around again, her blue eyes blazing. "'She's got a way with kids.' Excuse me. Because of you, Mr. Know-It-All, I have been assaulted by a pint-size bully, had catsup splattered all over my uniform, endured insults about my looks and my intelligence, and been accused of kidnapping."

She strode to the door, and not bothering to turn around, yelled, "I have wasted precious hours so you could play rescuer. Now I'm going home to sleep."

She slammed out, sending vibrations through his eardrums that only the roar of a jet engine could equal. He smiled. *What a woman.*

FLY ME

Shirley Ann Wilder

www.BOROUGHSPUBLISHINGGROUP.com

FLY ME
Copyright © 2014 Shirley Ann Wilder

ISBN 978-1-942886-24-2

To John, my gray eagle, who watches over us all, and my flying children: Captain Jim; his beautiful first officer, Sharon; and my amazing daughter Julie, who is so much more than an FA—she's truly a flying angel.

CONTENTS

FLY ME

Chapter 1

First Officer Ronnie Talbot circled the tail section of the B757, gazing up at the underbelly while shining her flashlight on critical areas of the aircraft. The fuel trucks had just arrived and orange-vested men unreeled large hoses that would supply the source of energy for this monster to climb thirty-five thousand feet while carrying close to two hundred souls.

Smoothing her hair into the neat bun, she repositioned her black uniform cap. It was uncomfortable to wear with her particular hairstyle, but professionalism was her goal, not comfort. If comfort was what she was after, she'd take out the pins and let her hair fall around her shoulders, free and easy. Oh, well. After boarding, she'd remove the hat. Satisfied that the plane was airworthy, she took the metal service stairs to the flight deck. Her black closed-toe pumps echoed each step to the entry.

Once inside the cabin, she slipped out of her jacket and hung it in the small compartment reserved for crew. Putting her hat on a hook behind the right seat, she donned her headset and began communications with ground personnel. Switching on the in-flight computer, she did routine checks while the system booted up and started flashing out data.

Comparing latest weather with earlier reports she'd fished from her flight bag, she made a few notations on her clip¬board. Scanning the checklist, she let her thoughts drift to the captain who'd been listed for this trip. She was a little worried—she'd heard plenty about Captain Farrell. He had a reputation of being a Don Juan and she'd had her fill of the type. Not that she couldn't handle him; God knows she'd had plenty of experience and knew the drill.

First they undress you with their eyes and think they've given you a compliment. Then they start with the small talk and the jokes, and that's supposed to loosen you up. The number of steps to seduction depends on how smooth the operator. And from what she'd heard about Captain Farrell, he was the smoothest.

He thought he was God's gift to every female and all skirts were supposed to swoon at his feet. Well, she had more important things to do with her life than let a man come between her and her goals. She'd come too far without any help—but with plenty of problems— from men.

~~~

Captain Trent Farrell, better known as Flip, rolled his brain bag down the corridor to Global Airlines operations entry. His dad would give him a bad time for having a "wussy" bag. But after eleven years of carrying forty pounds of required flight manuals, wheels made a lot more sense than they had when he'd first checked out as captain at the young age of twenty-four. Back then, lifting two eighty at the gym was not a problem. Punching in the access code, he entered dispatch, where the buzz of computers and ringing telephones dominated the airspace.

"Hey, Flip, how's it goin'?"

"Not too bad, Frank. What's the weather look like from here to Baltimore?"

"I haven't had a chance to pull it up yet, but I think your first officer already got the stats."

Flip popped his attention to the dispatcher. "Are you telling me Jack Larson checked in already?"

He was in shock. Jack was a hell of a pilot, but he hadn't made an early check-in on time since the Wright brothers launched their first flying machine. Flip glanced at his watch just to make sure it hadn't stopped. It was just now a quarter to six. There was still an hour and thirty-five minutes before takeoff.

Although the captain was only required to arrive an hour before flight, Flip made it a point to be the first to check in. While the fallout from 9/11 had added more preflight time to passengers, uniformed flight crews were checked through a special security gate. Flip was so well known he breezed through security without any added time.

Arriving early was just an old habit left over from his days as first officer. Jack normally buzzed in late, then transformed himself into a human dynamo until push off. At first, the tardiness had irked Flip, but Jack was so good at his job, it became easier to overlook and accept. So far, he'd never been so late that they'd had to delay a flight.

"Jack called in sick. You got a reserve by the name of "—Frank consulted the monitor screen—"R. Talbot."

Flip racked his brain, but couldn't place an R. Talbot. "I don't think I know him. What's he look like?"

"Don't know. I just came on duty so I didn't see him. I guess he's out doing the walk-around."

"I'll grab a cup of coffee first, then meet him in the aircraft."

Flip saw Global flight attendants Cindy Lee and Janet McCoy chattering as they pulled their wheels down the hall while juggling disposal cups of coffee.

"Hi, girls, long time no see."

Flip couldn't believe his luck. The two best friends worked well as a team in the cabin, which made things run smooth. When an emergency came up, experience and competency were what counted. The fact that they were both beautiful didn't hurt either. Although he could think it, he didn't dare say it. Sexual harassment laws had wiped out even the most innocent of compliments. He would be spending two long days and an overnight in Baltimore with them, and they could be a lot of fun. There was the little item of duty, but this trip could be very interesting.

"Hi, Flip." Cindy gave him a wide grin, displaying her deep dimples. She'd barely made it through flight attendant training, struggling to reach the overhead bins. Not to mention it was sometimes an even bet on who outweighed who—Cindy or the bag she had to stow in the overhead compartments. Chinese-American, petite, almond-eyed and gorgeous, Cindy had made it and was now a favorite with passengers and crew.

Janet's smile was not as broad as Cindy's, but carried its own message. "Hello, Flip, we meet again."

Flip had dated a lot of flight attendants along the way, but Janet McCoy—tall, willowy and sassy—had been the most dangerous.

With expectations and the talent to turn them into realities, she'd taught him things about women he hadn't even imagined existed. At the time he'd been grateful, but after she got possessive and demanding, her charm, in and out of bed, began to lose the sizzle and steam it had in the beginning.

It became clear to Flip that Janet wanted their relationship to advance past fun and games and into the marriage and family stage. Settling down with her, or anyone else, in the near future was not an option he cared to entertain at the present time. Janet was fun to date, but he didn't want to be a permanent member of the team. He'd managed to stay friendly with her while avoiding any deeper involvement. He'd been able to reach thirty-four on his last birthday with his bachelor status intact, and in spite of his mother's urging him to find a nice girl, Flip liked things just as they were.

Janet and Cindy shared a crash pad with four other flight attendants. Thoughts of all that feminine sexuality in one apartment were almost enough to make Flip forget he had to fly the next two days and keep his mind on a professional level. He always put safety at the top of the list and letting his mind wander off compromised that goal.

The trio headed toward the aircraft and he didn't miss any of the hints Janet threw at him regarding how much she'd missed seeing him the last few months. When they got to the gate, he let them board the plane as he made an excuse to confer with the ramp agent. Janet was way too aggressive. He'd have to be on guard or he'd find himself right back where he had been—being steered by her toward jewelry stores.

Flip stowed his bag as two more flight attendants hurried on board behind him. One of them was a sweet married gal with two kids; the other, a poster-board handsome guy. The bets were still out regarding his sexual preference.

Checking his watch again, Flip chided himself for not yet meeting his first officer. Letting two of the FAs squeeze by him to the galley, he tossed his empty coffee container in the trash and stepped through the door to the flight deck.

He didn't need to see the silky blonde bun at the nape of that slender neck to know this was not your run-of-the-mill copilot. The scent of gardenias or something equally pleasant wafted into his nostrils and alerted his senses with a shout of *female in cockpit*.

It wasn't that he wasn't aware of female pilots. In fact, he'd had a woman instructor when he was getting his multiengine rating—but she'd been older than his mother. A sturdy lady with corkscrew-permed gray hair and a tough-as-nails personality.

He knew the industry was changing, but this was too fast. He wasn't ready to have one in his cockpit—er, flight deck—yet. It was fine if they wanted to fly commuters or general aviation, but the majors? Not so fine.

This female could stop traffic and turn heads. He stood there enjoying the view as she leaned across her seat to check circuits and turn on required switches. Her profile was a study of perfection: Her small nose tilted just a bit; a provocative beauty mark decorated the area just above her full upper lip. Now he knew why the rampers had been grinning when they went about their jobs. This made any guy's job worth showing up for.

The goddess spun around and Flip found himself staring into eyes the color of an Indian summer sky. So blue it hurt to look at them because you might spin out and crash.

"Captain Farrell." She extended one perfectly mani¬cured hand. "Ronnie Talbot."

Even through the starched crisp uniform shirt, Flip could tell that underneath there had to be a flimsy piece of lace covering two glorious breasts. He wondered what it would take to make them pebble into hard sweet morsels. She wore slacks but they didn't hide the long firm limbs that tapered into slender ankles. He was disappointed to see feet in sensible low-heeled pumps—he'd been imagining a high-stepping number with an ankle strap. Flip's gaze traveled back up to her face, which now posed confusion.

"You are Captain Farrell, aren't you?"

His throat felt dry, and like an adolescent just brinking puberty, he croaked, "Yees."

"I mean, yes," he repeated in a deeper masculine tone. "Call me Flip." He gave her a smile that had been called dazzling by more than one woman who'd passed through his life at one time or another.

"I'm sorry, Captain. I wouldn't feel comfortable being on such familiar terms when I've just met you."

His grin was not returned. One look at her face made it clear there was no chance her response was a joke. She was strictly business.

The flight attendants greeted the passengers filing into the plane, most of them trying to peek a look at the pilots through the open door.

"When we're loaded, do you want me to do the radio or shall I take the first leg?"

Boy, she cuts to the chase. With his ego—both in his head and below the belt—severely squashed, he took his place in the left seat and reached for his headset.

Another emotion quickly replaced his lust: anger. It wasn't one he allowed himself to indulge at work because it kept him from doing his best. She'd caught him off guard. This is the problem letting women in the flight deck. Damn feminist movement had ruined a lot of good things and this was just about the worst.

Well, First Officer Talbot, since I don't know you either, we'll go by the book. My book.

"The captain always takes the first flight out, Talbot. Try to remember that and you won't get embarrassed stepping on any toes." Slipping on his dark glasses, Flip stole a sideways glance to see how the FO had reacted to his sharp reprimand. As far as he could tell, it didn't appear to have made an impression. Her expression remained cool and controlled. She went about second officer duties without a word or flaw in her performance. By the book—as if the FAA were on board.

Communication was confined to only what was necessary and as soon as all the passengers were reported on board, the flight deck door was closed and locked. Flip gave a wave to ground crew as they were pushed away from the gate and started to taxi toward the runway.

After they'd received clearance to take off and had climbed to their cruising altitude, Flip turned to the woman beside him. While he couldn't say much for her personality, he couldn't deny she was still the most beautiful copilot he'd ever had—not to mention frustrating as hell.

"Look, I'm sorry if I bit your head off. I'm not much on formalities." He decided to give her one more chance. Maybe she was nervous, although she'd displayed no hint of nerves when she made the routine announcements for the passengers' benefit. "Everyone calls me Flip."

She met his gaze and shrugged. "I suppose I did sound a bit straight-laced, but I was raised to be very respect¬ful. Flip doesn't sound like an appropriate name for a pilot."

Flip chuckled. "Well, I hate to admit it, but it's damned appropriate. At sixteen, I landed my dad's old taildragger in a marshy field. The damn thing ground-looped. The front wheels stuck in the mud and the tail came up and over, and there I was hanging upside down in my Dad's little Cessna 140. Thus the nickname Flip. It stuck."

"I certainly hope your landings have improved or I'll be glad to execute them for you."

Damn, she's got a one-track mind. Didn't she hear what I said?

Was she just about flying? Nothing else? Didn't she realize how goddamn cocky she sounded?

I've probably forgotten more than she'll ever know about flying or landing.

Flip felt the anger building again. What was it about her? She might be hot looking, but beauty couldn't count that much. This was just one of the problems that came from women invading a man's territory. In the cabin, females were perfect. They patted the pillows, served the meals and generally made the passengers feel safe and comfortable. Give them authority and stripes on their cuffs and you got the kind of iceberg he had sitting next to him.

He glanced at her quickly. Her classic cheekbones were delicately tinted with either embarrassment, which he doubted, or blusher from her makeup bag.

Hey, who needs this kind of crap? He reminded himself that he could have his pick of two beauties serving coffee and sodas in the cabin. Still, his anger ebbed just long enough for him to wonder what her hair looked like if it wasn't twisted up in that granny knot. How long was it and how would it look spread across a pillow? *His.*

~~~

What's the matter with you, Talbot? Ronnie gave herself a mental shake. Maybe the captain was trying to make amends, and she'd karate-chopped him with her words. *Would it be such a crime for you to be nice to him—even if he is a man?*

Her past had gotten in the way of her objectivity again. Not that he didn't have a reputation that called for caution, but she also knew gossip wasn't necessarily fact. And what she'd heard about Captain Farrell came right from the gossip mill.

She pretended she was looking at the many dials and switches in front of them both while at the same time managing a pretty good look at the man she'd just beaten into silence for the second time in less than thirty minutes.

There was no doubt in her mind Captain Trent Farrell, or Flip, as he preferred to be called, could easily catch the eye of most women without even trying. He wasn't a pretty boy but he had one of those square jaws with a cleft chin that had been hard to resist ever since Michael Douglas had romanced the stone and Kathleen Turner.

She judged him to be well over six feet because she'd had to look up at him when he'd entered the cockpit—oops, flight deck. She had to watch it, even mentally, that she didn't slip into the good-ole-boy slang of male pilots.

Since the industry had made some drastic changes by allowing women to become commercial pilots and actually fly left seat, lots of things had changed. No more centerfolds pasted on the inside covers of the regulation books, no more dumb-blonde jokes and no more *cockpit.*

Two quick taps broke the uncomfortable silence. Ronnie heard the key turn in the lock and saw a flight attendant squeeze through the entry.

"Just wanted to see what ya'll wanted to drink. Captain, do you still take your coffee black?"

"You got it, Marsha. How're the kids?"

"Meaner than rattlesnakes and twice as slippery." She giggled.

"Good. Boys should give their moms a run for the money. That's the way it's supposed to be. Makes coming to work more fun, huh?"

Ronnie watched the friendly encounter and wished she could do that. Maybe it was because the FA was married and wasn't a challenge to Flip.

Flip turned toward Ronnie. "Marsha has two of the cutest kids you've ever seen. How old are they now?" He swiveled his head to look at Marsha.

"Davy will be three next month and Benjamin was five in August. He started kindergarten this year and every morning Davy cries to go with him."

Still grinning, Marsha addressed Ronnie. "I'm sorry. We haven't met. I'm Marsha, lead FA today."

Ronnie returned her smile and stretched her hand across the space separating them. "Ronnie Talbot. It's nice to meet you, Marsha. You have my admiration for being able to do your job and still find time for raising children."

"Let's hold off on the admiration until Walt and I see if we can keep up with them until they're both in school. All day."

Marsha giggled again, but the praise had found its mark. Beaming, she asked, "What can I get for you, Ronnie: coffee, tea, soda?"

"Could I just have a cup of hot water? I have my own tea bag. It's an herbal tea that I special-order."

"Sure. You want any cream or sugar? Lemon?"

"No, just the hot water. Thanks a lot."

Silence hung heavily in the confined area as soon as Marsha shut the door.

~~~

"Marsha, did you meet the FO?" Janet was leaning against the galley sink, applying a new coat of bright red lipstick.

Marsha reached around Janet for the coffeepot and poured the hot fluid into one cup. "Yeah, she's nice. Wish I'd kept my shape as well as she has."

"Well, it's probably job security for her. To be a female jet jockey you have to get under a good man and work up. Can't do that unless you look good."

"You know, Janet, that's a nasty thing to say. Why don't you wait until you meet her before you spread gossip and rumors?"

Marsha filled the other Styrofoam cup, then set them both on a small tray. Squeezing past the redhead, she tapped on the flight deck door again.

~~~

Marsha returned with their drinks before the silence made the situation even more strained. Ronnie took the cup of hot water and gave the FA a full, warm smile. She even returned Flip's gaze with a slight smile. She wanted to show him that she was not the iceberg he probably thought she was. *I can be as friendly as anyone if he'd give me a chance.*

Ronnie was delegated to doing all the radio work, all the announcements, and wasn't allowed one landing the entire day. She saw signs of fatigue in Flip's mannerisms; he'd yawned at one point but never asked her to take over. The only time he'd left his station was when they'd arrived at their first destination, unloaded and picked up new passengers. He'd left the plane and gone into the terminal without saying a word to her. Ronnie assumed it was to relieve his bladder. She'd made a trip to the aircraft lavatory after her cup of tea, but she'd had the courtesy to inform him that she'd be leaving the flight deck to go to the cabin for a few minutes.

Ronnie saw that Flip wasn't going to make the first move. He was such a typical macho male that it probably hadn't occurred to him that she might be nervous. Her little attempt at a joke had fallen completely flat. If he weren't so full of himself, he'd have seen she was just kidding about making the landings for him. Okay, she'd make another attempt at small talk.

"So, you've been flying for quite a while. Started at sixteen?"

"Fourteen. Legally at sixteen," he answered curtly.

"Of course, you said your father had a plane. That would make it easier. Having a plane at your disposal, I mean."

She nibbled at her bottom lip. He wasn't making it any easier, but she couldn't blame him. After several awkward moments, the same silence pact was reestablished—conver¬sation was limited to job necessity only. She'd acted way too self-assured. If he only knew how deep her insecurities ran. But that was something she'd never tell anyone, least of all this Captain Macho.

She'd learned how to fool most people while still in her teens. Strutting across a stage she'd smiled until her face hurt and they awarded her "Miss" whatever contest her mother had entered her in at the time. She'd hated every minute of it, but the prize money paid for school. Otherwise she'd be stuck in a dead-end job just like Mom. Or even worse, hooked up with some guy who thought you ought to kiss up to him because he bought you a few trinkets—again, just like her mom.

Ronnie was more grateful for having been blessed with brains than good looks. An aeronautical engineering degree in addition to the commercial ratings was evidence of her intelligence. She could fly as good as any man, even better than some. She knew procedures backward and forward—every check ride and ground school test score was solid proof. She never let down her guard; she took nothing for granted.

It was a big relief when the last leg of the trip was over and the crew boarded the courtesy van for the hotel.

"Cindy and I are headed for Leonardo's. Anybody want to join us for dinner?"

Ronnie couldn't miss the implication in Janet's not-so-subtle glance in Flip's direction. She watched as Flip responded with a big smile, much like the one he'd greeted her with just this morning.

"Sure, I'll be your escort. Rigatoni or lasagna sounds really good. What else is on the menu?"

"You never can tell, Captain. You might be in for a surprise." Cindy giggled and Janet jabbed her in the ribs while giving Flip another long look.

Ronnie didn't know if she should speak up or wait to be invited. It was obvious the girls only extended the invitation for Flip's benefit.

"Well, don't count on me," Marsha piped up from her seat in front of Ronnie. "I'm hitting the sack. I seldom sleep through the night when I'm home. One of the boys always wants a drink of water or Walt gets called for emergency duty." She stretched her arms out in front of her. "We don't have to report until eleven tomorrow. I'm sleeping until ten."

The male flight attendant made an excuse about not feeling up to it either, and Ronnie felt the attention shift to her. She didn't mistake the chill in Janet's gaze that seemed to say, *Don't even think about it.*

Not even daring to look at Flip, she quickly stated, "Oh, I'm ordering in. I wanted to go over some notes. I have recurrent ground school scheduled soon. Thanks anyway."

She could almost hear Janet's sigh of relief. Well, fine, let her entertain the egotistical, chauvinistic jet jockey. Ronnie turned to look out the window and watch the bustle of the Baltimore streets as the van continued to their overnight quarters.

God, she was tired of being alone. Why couldn't she make friends with Marsha? She would even have been happy to share dinner with the male FA, but he obviously had other plans too. This was the price she paid for not com¬promising her standards. Eventually it was going to pay off, and she would be something more than Miss Citrus or Miss Central Valley—she'd be Captain Talbot.

~~~

Flip stepped out of the shower, toweled off and slipped into clean clothes. He didn't feel like dinner, especially with two young beauties who thought flying was still the way to snag a rich husband. Besides he couldn't put Ronnie's face out of his mind. She'd looked sad and lost. He couldn't help but remember when she'd smiled at Marsha and even slightly at him. He'd thought at that moment the icy blonde could thaw after all and wondered what had turned her into the glacial goddess. He'd been ready to insist she come along, but after giving her the cold shoulder all day and acting like a bastard, he didn't think she'd accept the invite. Not letting her fly all day had been really stupid. He was beat. His neck felt like he had whiplash and the muscles in his shoulders were bunched in knots. He should go to the gym and work off the tension instead of putting a ton of carbs into his system.

He ran a comb through his hair, peering closer into the mirror for any sign of gray. So far he'd only had a few, but his dad retired with a full head of silver hair. This business could do that to you. Some said you age two years for every year you fly.

He couldn't imagine Ronnie ever aging. A mental image of her floated in front of the mirror. He couldn't erase from his mind how sad she'd looked, or how beautiful. Even after the long day, every hair was in place, her eyes were still enchanting, and the face was a work of art.

He vowed that tomorrow he was turning over a new leaf. He'd extend the olive branch. He prided himself on getting along with his crew. He might as well get resolved to the fact that female pilots were a sign of the times. And he couldn't deny this particular one interested him.

He would need to turn on his charm full speed, but he had decided: The ice princess would thaw. He was at expert at heating up women—this one would just take a little more time and finesse.

Chapter 2

Flip shifted his weight from one foot to the other. This was ridiculous. Everyone was here and the van driver was getting restless. Everyone, that is, except First Officer Talbot. He walked from the curbside to the wide glass walls and peered inside to the lobby, hoping to see Ronnie exiting the elevator.

Janet stuck her head out of the van and yelled, "Come on, Flip. It's her problem. Let's go before we're all late."

Pulling open the heavy glass door, Flip turned around, frowned and spat out the words, "I can't fly without a copilot."

He strode across the lobby to the clerk behind the counter. Interrupting the man's phone conversation, Flip said, "Please ring Global Airline employee Talbot, fourth floor, and tell her she's late."

Irritation showing through his thin-lipped smile, the red-jacketed employee answered, "Miss Talbot, sir, checked out over an hour ago. She took the van with an earlier group of airport passengers."

Flip spun on his heel and crossed the large marble-floored lobby in a matter of seconds. Wrenching the door open, he leaped into the waiting van. "Let's go," Flip growled, folding his arms across his chest and turning to stare out the window.

"Where's Ronnie? Are we leaving her?" Cindy's questions tumbled out as the driver pulled away from the curb.

"The ice princess left on the early van." Flip grabbed the newspaper from the seat. From the corner of his eye, Flip caught the nudge Janet gave her friend's shoulder.

Silence, except for the occasional sound of newspaper sheets being turned, settled inside the van like the mist gathering on the vehicle's windshield.

Godammit, she'd done it again. Succeeded in getting him all pissed off when he'd made a pact with himself to be nice. This was the day he was going to be friendly and give her another chance to be human instead of an icicle.

The ride to the airport took longer than usual. The traffic, slowed by an accident, seemed destined to be held to a crawl. Flip began to regret the minutes he'd wasted waiting for the inconsiderate Talbot. Janet was right: They'd be late if they didn't speed up soon.

~~~

Now what is the matter with him? Ronnie had once again failed to get Captain Farrell to warm up.

She'd put her best foot forward by getting to the airport ahead of schedule and doing all the grunt work like pulling up weather reports, doing the walk around and checking with reservations for any unusual passengers. They were scheduled to have one unaccompanied minor on board, but Marsha was an expert with kids so that really wasn't a problem.

She'd given him a full rundown only to have him recheck everything she'd reported, even going to the trouble to repeat the weather forecasts. Frankly, she was getting tired of Captain Farrell's arrogant attitude.

The takeoff out of Baltimore was uneventful and as soon as they reached altitude, the clouds and mist were replaced by sunny blue skies. Ronnie glanced over at Flip, who'd donned his usual shades. She had a feeling he hid behind the dark glasses so she couldn't tell where his gaze was focused.

"Captain, am I going to get an opportunity to fly today?" She'd had enough. She'd been patient and professional, and he was being petty. His male ego just couldn't stand the thought that a woman could do his job.

"Of course, Talbot. I fully intended for you to fly yesterday, but I was afraid that rod you've been sitting on might cause you even more discomfort."

"What? What rod?" Then she realized he'd been making a snide remark. Should she ignore it? Could she? Nope.

"Excuse me, Captain, but who whizzed in your cheerios?" Tit for tat was her motto. Her gaze locked onto his profile. "I've done every¬thing in my power to impress you and you treat me like a— a—an idiot."

Flip's head spun toward her, and even with his dark glasses, she could feel the daggers aimed at her.

"Oh, you impressed me all right," he almost snarled the words. "I was impressed when I stood on the curb outside the hotel waiting for you to get your ass down¬stairs to the van. I was further impressed when I rushed to the counter to have them ring your room, only to be told by the snot-nosed desk clerk that you'd already left for the airport." He ripped his glasses off and his steely gray eyes, like drills, bored holes through her.

"Are you interested in my impressions?" he continued. "My impression is that you're a spoiled-rotten daddy's girl who got bored with the country club scene and got the old man to lay out the bucks for some university that offers an aviation program. Lucky for you, you do have brains or you'd never have made it through, but as for your skills in assisting and cooperating with crew members—your CMR—lady you flunk on all points."

Tears welled in the corners of Ronnie's eyes and she fought to keep them from sliding down her cheeks. For a moment, she was speechless. My God, what had she been thinking? Of course she should have notified her captain of her plans. But as for CRM—did he think he was a star at crew resource management?

"You're absolutely correct, Captain. I should have notified you of my intentions. I apologize."

Ronnie kept her expression as solemn as she could and was surprised when Flip's irritation with her seemed to lose some of its power. He stuck his glasses into his shirt pocket and glanced in her direction, his frown no longer present. "Don't worry about it. I chalked it off as rookie error." He unbuckled his seat harness. "I'll be in the back for a few minutes." Ronnie watched him get up and at the door he hesitated. "It's on autopilot, but you're in charge. Buzz if you need me."

Ronnie couldn't believe what had just taken place. As fast as his anger had flamed, it seemed to fizzle just as quickly. She was glad she hadn't tried to defend herself. He wouldn't believe it anyway. How could she tell him that she'd spent every cent she'd ever made smiling at cameras on her college tuition and then for flying lessons?

He had no idea of what her life had been like. Her mother always chasing some rainbow, and the dumps they'd lived in. She hadn't even seen the inside of a country club until one of the beauty contests had been held there. He could think what he chose. He'd been unfair, but she was relieved he hadn't seen the tears that had almost escaped.

She toyed with the idea of disengaging the autopilot, but decided she better not push her luck. He could still make trouble for her. He was obviously well liked by crews while she was still relatively unknown.

~~~

Flip stepped into the forward restroom and stared into the small mirror. "Well, are you proud of yourself? Big man in the cockpit can make little girls cry. What an ass you are."

He hung his head and pushed on the water. Quickly cupping his hands before the tap automatically cut off, he splashed his face.

Ripping a paper towel from the dispenser, he dried off and opened the door.

"Hey, Marsha, could I get a cup of hot water and one of coffee?" Flip entered the galley area, where Marsha was loading a tray with Styrofoam cups and pitchers of coffee.

"Flip, you didn't have to come back here. I'd have been up there in just a few minutes." She gave him one of her customary smiles and filled the requested cups. Adding napkins as she handed them to him, she looked up quizzically. "Everything okay up there?"

"Oh God, Marsha, who knows?" He accepted the cups and then leaned one shoulder against the aircraft wall. "Tell me, Marsha: Am I hard to get along with? Do I put people off? What kind of a reputation do I have among crews?"

"You're asking me?" Marsha looked surprised. "Flip, you're a friend who plays poker with my husband and loves my kids. I think you're great."

"Well, you hear talk—what do others think?"

"Jack Larsen thinks you hung the moon." She leaned forward, nodded toward the main cabin and whispered. "Both girls and maybe Alan too," she teased, "want to get you in bed."

"Seriously, Marsh. Don't mess with me."

"Boy, she does have you in a dither." The expression on her round face sobered. "Okay, the general feeling is that you're a good, safe pilot who can hold his own in any emergency. We all like that."

She spoke with an honesty that Flip knew he could trust. "The other thing is that you're a player. You like to travel fast, both in the air and with the ladies. Since I'm deliriously happy with Walt and not interested in scoring points, I just think you're one of the good guys."

Flip took a moment to let it all sink in, then smiled. "Thanks…I think. Uh, could you open the door to the flight deck?" He gestured with his two cup-filled hands to the locked door.

"Sure." Marsha squeezed past him, inserted her key, then stepped back. He grinned his thanks and entered the flight deck.

"Break time. One cup hot water and one cup awful coffee."

It pleased him to see that he'd surprised Ronnie. She almost looked scared. Her incredible blue eyes sparkled and her full lips tilted upward into a small smile that slowly expanded, showing her perfect white teeth.

"Thank you so much." She sat the cup down and fished around in her case for her special teabag.

"So, where do you get that tea?" He could have cared less, but he wanted to engage in some sort of small talk, any kind, just to undo some of the damage between them.

There was something about her he found irresistible. It wasn't just that she was beautiful. She'd reminded him of a little girl when he'd almost made her cry. She wasn't a spoiled brat; he sensed that now. No, something in her past must have hurt her bad for her put up such a thick wall of ice. She sipped her tea and went into detail about some of the other health foods she prescribed to daily.

He knew so little about her, and if Jack got over whatever bug he had, he'd be back to finish out the month's schedule. For the first time, Flip actually hoped his buddy Jack had some rare African plague—nothing serious, just something to keep him on sick leave until Flip could get to know Ronnie better.

But that still wouldn't guarantee Ronnie would get put on his flights, he thought. There were lots of reserve copilots. Unless he could pull some strings. Whom did he know on scheduling? But it was a moot subject. Jack had never even been to Africa.

The remainder of the flight went better than Flip could have hoped. He kept Ronnie totally amused about some of his early flying attempts, and the wistful look on her face when he'd talked about his family had not gone unnoticed.

She laughed so hard she was in tears, as he told her the story of his mother chasing him up a tree.

"I couldn't believe my mother could still climb a tree. She's so old, I thought. I realized years later that if I was ten at the time, my mother was the ripe old age of thirty-three, younger than I am now."

He glanced over at the pretty girl still chuckling and wiping her eyes. He wanted to ask her about her family, but he'd been so nasty earlier and they were starting to get final approach instructions. Things got busy and a business-like atmosphere returned to the flight deck.

Trying to sound nonchalant, Flip asked, "Have you made the approach into San Diego?"

"As a matter of fact, I have. I had my on-line training in and out of here for several flights. I had a trip last week that ended up here, but I don't think the captain trusted me to land."

"Well, I've watched you now for a while. I think you can do it." Flip usually did all the landings into San Diego with new pilots because it was not your open plains, out-in-the-boondocks airport.

Incoming pilots had to make a steeper-than-normal approach over a park¬ing garage, urban neighborhoods and across several freeways before setting down at Lindbergh International Airport. He only hoped his instincts were right about this girl. He'd seen seasoned pilots sweat as they skimmed by less than two hundred feet over the last building in the approach path.

After approach switched the aircraft over to tower control and landing clearance had been given, Flip watched Ronnie as he read the final checklist. Ronnie responded to each item confidently and with all the serenity of Mother Teresa.

He, on the other hand, could feel small drops of moisture gathering on his upper lip and forehead. It was difficult for him to sit back with a hands-off policy. He hoped she didn't make them go around because he wasn't about to give her more than one chance to do it right.

The landing was perfect, scarcely a bump as the jet rolled down the runway toward the taxiway and their gate.

Shutting down the engines, Flip spoke into the mike to make the welcome announcement. He then turned to Ronnie. "Could I buy you a drink? A healthy one of course. You made a great landing."

"Thanks. I appreciate the compliment." Pausing, she considered his offer, then answered, "I've been known to indulge in a glass of wine now and then." Giving him a full smile, she reached for her hat.

Flip released an inaudible sigh of relief and quipped, "Red or white?"

"It depends. But it's been a long trip. I think I need something hearty, robust, with a strong bouquet. Red, I think." She tilted her head and looked upward at the headliner. "Maybe a Cabernet would be nice."

Flip grinned, but he felt out of his league. All he knew about wine was color. Red or white. What else was there to know? He'd been thinking more along the lines of a cold beer and pretzels at the Nineteenth Hole, his favorite hangout near the golf course. Beer was healthy—made from grain, wasn't it?

He retrieved both jackets, shrugged into his, then helped Ronnie into hers as they rolled their bags toward the terminal.

"Flip, I was afraid you'd already taken off. Thank goodness, you're still here."

"What's the problem, Marsh? Hey there, cowboy, where'd you park your horse?"

The small boy clinging to Marsha's hand wore a tag on his jacket lapel, and a small red plastic backpack hung from his shoulders. He'd pulled his straw cowboy hat down almost to his eyebrows. The large brown eyes peering up at them reminded Flip of the chocolate drops his mom made every Christmas.

Flip squatted down to the little boy's level and fished into his pocket for a roll of Life Savers. This must be the unaccompanied minor Ronnie had mentioned. "Here, buddy, knock yourself out." The small cowboy grinned shyly and took the candy from Flip.

Marsha threw her arms up in a wild gesture and addressed Ronnie. "The father was supposed to be at the gate to meet the flight."

"Poor little guy." Flip watched Ronnie lean over and assist the youngster in unwrapping the candy roll. "What do you want me to do, Marsha?"

"Well, normally I'd wait to deliver him to the designated person, but Walt just buzzed me on my cell. Davy's running a temperature; it's probably another ear infection. I really need to get home."

"Hey, I'll hang until his dad shows up." He turned to focus his attention on Ronnie and the boy, who were compar¬ing Life Saver flavors. "Sorry, Ronnie. I guess I'll have to issue a rain check on that drink."

Ronnie straightened the cowboy hat so the small face was more visible and looked up at Flip. "I'll stay, too. Bobby was telling me all about the puppy his daddy is going to get. And did you know that Bobby is only four, but his mommy told the lady he was already five?"

Marsha groaned. "Oh, boy, someone screwed up big time. They should have asked for proof of age."

Marsha gratefully accepted Flip and Ronnie's offer, and adding a hopeful lilt to her voice, said, "I'm sure his dad will be along soon."

Flip and Ronnie watched Bobby wave good-bye as Marsha slung her purse over her shoulder and pulled her luggage toward the exit.

"I'll understand if you have to leave, Ronnie. I'll stay with Bobby."

"Actually, I'd like to hang around until the dad gets here. What were his parents thinking, letting a baby like this travel alone?"

"I'm not a baby. I get to go to kindergarten next year." Bobby shoved Ronnie at knee level with both hands.

Ronnie's legs momentarily buckled and she lunged in Flip's direction. He stopped her fall and grabbed both her upper arms.

"Hey, Bobby, you don't shove a lady. She didn't mean you were really a baby—that means she thinks you're a good-looking cowboy. Right, Ronnie?"

Regaining her footing, she straightened and looked down at the pint-sized bully, who was trying his best to scowl at the adults while his lower lip quivered.

"Of course I knew right away he was a big boy."

Flip, while in no hurry to let go of Ronnie, finally slid one hand down to her wrist, lacing his fingers with hers; he offered the other one to the boy. "Bet you're getting hungry, huh?"

Nodding, Bobby fought back tears dangerously close to spilling down his small face. "Do you think my daddy got lost? He just moved here and maybe he doesn't know the way to get me."

"Well, don't you worry about it. I'm going to look on your tag there and we'll find out what happened jiffy quick."

Bobby's face lightened and he grinned wide. "Lady, I'm sorry I pushed you."

Ronnie slipped her hand out of Flip's grasp and knelt down in front of the child. "That's okay. You ought to see what I do when I get mad."

Flip joined Ronnie at the boy's eye level, his thigh pressing against hers as he nonchalantly placed one hand on her knee. "No, Bob, trust me—you don't want to see that."

Ronnie rolled her eyes. "I beg your pardon? Is this coming from Mr. Congeniality?"

Flip returned her smile and reached for the tag pinned to Bobby's jacket. Included in the plastic tag holder were two luggage claim checks.

"There's two phone numbers here and two names. Guess we better call someone. It's been long enough." Putting one hand under her elbow, he helped Ronnie to her feet.

"Okay, Bob, first we give your dad a buzz; then we eat. How does that sound?"

The youngster did a series of small jumps in place and shouted, "Good. Can I have French fries with double catsup? Mommy thinks they're no good, but they are."

"You bet, cowboy." Flip leaned closer to Ronnie and whispered, "Take him in the coffee shop and order whatever he wants. I'll make the calls and join you in a few."

~~~

Bobby was making tracks in the puddle of catsup on his plate with each French fry before popping it into his mouth from the height of an arm's length above his head. The hamburger sat untouched except for a single bite showing the imprint of miniature teeth.

Ronnie, giving in to her stomach growls, ordered a salad with vinaigrette dressing and a bottle of mineral water. She would have ordered something for Flip, but had no idea what he liked. He'd been gone quite a while and she didn't know what to do with a little kid. They made her nervous. As an only child, she'd been more comfortable with grownups.

She looked up, relieved, when she saw Flip scanning the coffee shop, and waved to attract his attention. He nodded as he wove his way around the small Formica tables to her booth.

His stride was long and she tried to imagine how those muscular legs looked in a pair of shorts. Carrying his jacket, he'd undone the first three buttons on his shirt and discarded his epaulets and tie. The muscles in his broad shoulders rippled as he maneuvered his wheels; two bright yellow bags had been added to the top of his flight case. He rolled the baggage expertly around the tables and other diners.

His thick hair was a deep, rich brown until the light caught it just a certain way, then auburn streaks flashed through it. Ronnie usually didn't let herself give such a once-over to any guy, but she'd spent the better part of almost three days with this man and it didn't hurt to appreciate pleasant scenery.

Bobby was now making bombs out of small potato scraps, letting them drop into the blobs of catsup. Flip started to sit next to the boy, then reassessed the mess and squeezed in next to Ronnie.

"We've got a problem. No one is answering at either number. I've called crew scheduling and no one knows what to do. This has never happened before. Everyone in the front office went home at five o'clock. It's now past seven, Pacific Time. In Baltimore, it's less than an hour until midnight.

Flip glanced at Bobby slumped in the booth. The cowboy hat hung from its cord off one small shoulder. Red smears of catsup decorated the face and shirt, with a fair portion congealed in clumps on the table. The brown eyes were now almost hidden by thick-lashed lids. Bobby blinked, then closed his eyes. Scooting out of the booth, Flip said softly, "This kid needs to find a bed."

Following, Ronnie yawned, looked at her watch and answered, "The kid's not the only one."

Anytime, babe. I've got a king big enough for two. Chasing the wicked thought from his mind, Flip organized the luggage and took a few minutes to wipe some of the mess from Bobby's face. He hoisted the sleeping bundle up to his shoulder, shifting the weight until the small head nestled in the hollow of his neck.

"Where are we going?" Ronnie pulled her luggage and carried Bobby's bright red backpack and cowboy hat as she trailed behind Flip out of the coffee shop. "We can't leave the airport with this child."

Flip stopped abruptly and faced Ronnie. "Listen, I've always found it easier to ask forgiveness than seek permission." Keeping

Bobby firmly secure in his grasp, he readjusted his load with his free hand, then continued toward the exit. "Frankly, I don't relish sitting up all night in the terminal until some errant parent remembers he had a kid coming to visit."

"What kind of car do you drive?" Flip asked as they walked toward the employee parking lot.

"I've got a Toyota sedan. Why?"

"Because I drove a classic two-seater MG roadster and it's not very accommodating for luggage. I usually put my bags in the front seat. Could you drive us to my house so I can put this kid to bed?"

"Oh sure, I guess. What if somebody turns up looking for him? Shouldn't we call the police or social services or someone? I don't think it's a good idea to leave the premises."

"I left word on the message machine at both numbers and also at the ticket counter. In a few hours things are going to be shutting down at the airport. Something definitely went wrong with picking up this kid. I've notified enough people and I am not staying here any longer."

"What are you going to do with your car?"

"It'll be okay. I've got a cover on it. No worse than another overnighter."

Flip thought it odd that Ronnie seemed surprised when he'd asked for a ride. Either she didn't know the size of classic vehicles or it hadn't occurred to her that one of them had to take the kid home. She hadn't offered.

He had the next three days off, but he sure hoped someone would claim Bobby by tomorrow. It'd be a shame if they had to call in social services. The little guy had already been through enough. What was it with parents? Didn't they know kids weren't a piece of luggage that could be claimed whenever they felt like it? Maybe that's why so many bags and kids got lost.

~~~

Ronnie watched as Flip settled the little boy in the huge bed. He hadn't bothered to undress Bobby for fear of waking him up. The ecru pillowcase now sported a sticky streak of red as Bobby burrowed his face deep into the pillow and made little snuffling sounds.

She scanned the room and noted with approval that the décor was tasteful. She hadn't known quite what to expect, but from the rumors she'd heard about Captain Farrell, it wouldn't have surprised her to see a mirror-covered ceiling.

A large desk with a computer and state-of-the-art equipment occupied one corner of the room while a small television sat on top of the triple-sized dresser.

The opposite wall held family photos and all kinds of airplane pictures. A large framed color shot caught her eye. Centered was a handsome couple; the man had silver hair and both were deeply tanned. Two tall young men with identical grins and cleft chins flanked them on each side. In front was a girl, shorter and younger than all the rest, with a sassy look and a thick mop of auburn curls. They were standing in front of a Cessna 140 taildragger that looked to be of the 1940s vintage. The girl was holding a certificate and grinning from ear to ear.

Ronnie felt Flip's presence behind her. He leaned over and rested his chin on her shoulder. He smelled good. Not like he'd bathed in aftershave or men's cologne, but a clean smell of shampoo, soap and just plain masculine hunk. If she didn't watch herself, she'd do something stupid—like swoon.

"I take it this is your family." She turned and dis¬lodged his chin because she wasn't sure if she could trust herself to have him so close.

"Yep. Pop, Mom and the sibs. The short one is Gloria. She'd just soloed—it was her sixteenth birthday."

"Your sister flies, too?" Ronnie was stunned. She'd been treated like a pariah when she'd tried to break into the ranks of the high and mighty. More people than she cared to remember had tried their best to discourage her. Her mother wanted her to be in show business or marry a rich man and forget the foolishness of being a pilot.

"Are you kidding? She didn't pursue flying as a career, but Gloria was worse than Mike or me when it came to sneaking Dad's plane out. She was the one who stole the hanger key and had spares made—then bribed Mike and me to teach her the basics in exchange for one."

"It's hard to believe that she got encouragement." Ronnie shook her head. "The first lesson I tried to take, the instructor took one look at me and told me that if God intended women to fly, He'd have made the sky pink."

Flip silently agreed with that instructor, but knew better than to voice it. He might not have felt that way if he could forget the lady instructor who almost got his sister killed. Gloria had been too eager to catch up with her brothers and on her own had hired this woman who had Gloria taking short cuts that could have been fatal. Not remembering to check the fuel for one. And when Gloria came in with the engine sputtering, it had scared her so badly, she'd never pursued flying past getting her private. But instead of voicing his feelings that some women should stay firmly on the ground, he said, "Actually, there are times at sunset when I've seen the sky look pink." Her smile assured him that he'd made the right decision.

Flip placed one hand high on Ronnie's shoulder, his thumb gently rubbing the soft area just behind her ear. When she turned, he slowly lowered his head and claimed her lips. They were just as he expected, sweet, but had an added tangy taste of something he couldn't identify. He deepened his kiss, and for a moment he felt her yield, then stiffen and pull back. He removed his hand when she retreated farther toward the door.

"I really should be going. I'm tired and it's getting late."

"I still owe you a glass of wine." He saw confusion in her eyes and wondered if she was that inexperienced.

"No, I can't stay. Thanks anyway." She was already halfway down the hall. "I'll leave my cell number and you let me know about Bobby."

"You're off until when?"

"Like you, I've got three days." She stopped at the front door, turned and smiled. "Thanks for letting me do the landing tonight. It meant a lot."

"No problem. But I'm still going to buy you that drink."

Chapter 3

Ronnie inspected the red splotches on her uniform, crammed it into the mesh bag that hung on the doorknob and made a mental note to go by the dry cleaners tomorrow. She tossed the remainder of her dirty laundry into the hamper and stepped into the shower.

The hot water felt good as she rotated the nozzle and the streams took turns pulsating the tired muscles in her back and shoulders. She'd held her emotions and actions in tight control all day. Now her stiff, aching body screamed in protest. She'd almost let go and given into her impulses when Flip's strong, gentle hands stroked her neck. She'd wanted to relax into his arms and lose herself in the fantasy: one where he was honorable, in love with her. One where she never had to anything to prove.

Get real, Ronnie. You know men better than that. They all had an agenda. Even today, she knew she was under the microscope. Big deal he let her land the plane. She'd been aware of the sweat popping out on his forehead. He didn't fool her one bit. One false move and he'd have taken over the controls so quick, she wouldn't have known what hit her.

Feeling some of the tension ease, Ronnie poured shampoo into her hair and scrubbed vigorously until it tingled. She conditioned, rinsed and then turned off the faucet. Stepping out of the shower, she wrapped one towel around her hair and a second around her torso.

It seemed stupid to blow-dry and style her hair, but she'd never been able to go to bed without doing it. Her mother had engraved it on her brain. "You never know, dear. If you have a fire drill, you'll want to look your best. Cameras are everywhere. A star can't be too careful."

Her mother was convinced that the airline gig was just something to fill in until Ronnie hit the big time in show biz. Ronnie had never bothered to set her straight. But maybe she should. She was almost thirty years old and it was high time she stood up to her mother.

Slipping into her thick, terrycloth robe, she went into the compact living room and poured herself a glass of Cabernet from the bottle sitting on the wet bar counter. It wouldn't hurt to have something to insure total relaxation, and she'd been craving a glass of wine ever since Flip's offer.

The deep red fluid slid down her throat and warmed from the inside out. It seemed to take the last of the sharp edges off her nerves and she finally felt at ease. She ambled over to the sectional sofa and plopped down in one corner.

"Damn, forgot to put it back on the stand again." Lifting the portable phone from the large glass cocktail table, she checked to see if it was holding the charge. It had been sitting there on the table since she'd been gone. For as much as she was organized, the portable phone was the one thing she always neglected. She didn't know why.

She punched in the numbers on her cell and listened to her voicemail messages. One from her mother, of course. One from her accountant. And then she noticed she'd also received a phone call directly to her cell. It had just come in not more than twenty minutes ago—from Flip.

It was too late to call her accountant and her mother could wait. She punched in Flip's number. He surprised her by picking up on the first ring.

"Hello?"

"Flip, this is Ronnie. What's the emergency?"

"Ronnie, you aren't going to believe this. Bobby's daddy called and he's coming over here with the cops."

"The police? I told you we should have called them."

Ronnie heard something akin to panic in Flip's voice. "He practically accused me of kidnapping his son. He called me a pervert. Can you get over here real quick?"

"Well, yes, but what can I do?"

"You can vouch for me. Tell them I'm not a child molester or a pornographer. This could get ugly. I think I could be in real trouble."

"I told you we shouldn't have left the airport."

"Okay, okay, you were right. Can you please come over here?"

She replaced the phone and reluctantly went to her closet. She was exhausted, but pulled out a pair of slacks and a red silk blouse. If he'd listened to her, he wouldn't be facing a possible morals or kidnapping charge. The few sips of wine had relaxed her just enough that she hoped she wouldn't fall asleep on the drive to Flip's house.

~~~

Flip had barely shown Ronnie to the leather wingback chair in his living room when the doorbell rang.

"Don't they care if they wake the boy? Dammit, you try to do a good deed and they want to arrest you for it." He pulled open the door and faced two uniformed officers and a young man wearing a tweed jacket.

"Trenton Maxwell Farrell?"

"That's me." He cringed inwardly at hearing his full name. It brought back memories of being raked over the coals by his mom or dad when he was twelve years old. Only for the most serious offenses was his full name invoked.

"I'm Officer Barnes and this is Officer Miller with the San Diego Police Department." The officer indicated the third member of their group with a nod of his head. "We're accompanied by John Weber, the father of the boy I understand you have in your custody."

Ronnie joined Flip at the doorway. Flip turned and snaked his arm around her waist, hooking his thumb in the belt of her gray slacks, pulling her closer. It wouldn't hurt to show that his preferences ran to beautiful adult women, not little boys.

"And the young lady is?"

"Who cares?" John Weber, standing slightly behind the policemen, looked as if he were about to burst. He glared at Flip with hostility, his forehead a mass of furrows and his mouth drawn into a tight, straight line. "I want this man arrested and I want my boy," he snapped. The older, burly cop restrained him when he lunged at Flip.

"Simmer down, Mr. Weber. We told you we'd take care of this."

"This is Miss Talbot," Flip said. Looking squarely at the distraught father, he added, "The first officer on Bobby's flight tonight."

"May we come in?" The younger of the two cops nodded at the door.

"Of course, if you can guarantee this man isn't going to try an impersonation of Mike Tyson."

"I just want to know what you've done with my kid."

"Mr. Weber"—Ronnie held out her hand—"it's a pleasure to meet you. Bobby seems like a wonderful little boy. I assure you he's just fine."

The man ignored her gesture of politeness and barged into the room. One of the policemen gripped him by the shoulder and stopped his progress. "Take it easy. We're going to go at this calmly."

They were finally all seated, and Flip and Ronnie re¬counted the details of how they happened to end up with Bobby Weber.

"Normally, I would have turned him over to the authorities but he just looked so tired and scared, and he'd developed a fondness for Miss Talbot."

Flip gave Ronnie a quick hug and grinned at her, ignoring the surprise that registered in her expressive blue eyes. "She has a way with kids."

Turning back to his visitors, he held his hands palms up to indicate his innocence. "What were we supposed to do? The kid was hungry and tired. So were we. No one showed up. The offices at Social Services were closed.

"In hindsight, I realize I should have notified the police immediately. Then maybe the charge would be child abandonment and Mr. Weber would be the one questioned." Flip ran his hand through his hair and glanced at Ronnie for moral support. She stood with folded arms across her chest. Stoic. She'd returned to the frosty blonde once more. Not a hint of warmth or understanding directed his way.

Flip redirected his attention back to the officer. "The kid looked exhausted and I figured we could sort all this out in the morning when Global operations or Social Services opened for business. After a fourteen hour day, it's hard to think straight."

Flip gestured toward the arched hallway. "Bobby's fine. He's sound asleep in the bedroom."

"Charley," Officer Barnes said to his partner, "go on back and check on the kid." Bobby's father also jumped to his feet, but Charley stopped him.

"Don't worry, Mr. Weber. I'll bring him out in just a few minutes."

Mr. Weber reluctantly sat back down and his gaze continued to drill holes through Flip.

Ignoring the angry looks, Flip asked in a voice heavy with sarcasm, "Officer Barnes, might I inquire why Mr. Weber is just now finding time to pick up his son?"

"It's none of your damn business, but if you must know Bobby's mother is a blonde, an idiot like all of them. She doesn't think about time zones."

Flip caught the flash of anger in Ronnie's eyes and noticed that Officer Barnes looked embarrassed that he was there representing the surly, rude man.

Officer Miller returned from the bedroom. "Pete, the kid's sleeping like a log. He's fully clothed except for shoes, and from the looks of his face, he enjoyed dinner."

"Mr. Weber, we have two choices here. We can take Bobby down to County General, have him checked out medically to be sure he's suffered no harm. Then he'd be placed at the children's center until we check out your record and that of your former wife to decide if Bobby is being cared for properly."

"Of course," Officer Miller said, entering the conver¬sation his partner had begun, "the fact that you were late and didn't even check on the flight until the boy had been here for hours won't look good."

"I told you. It was a mix-up. Helen, my ex, knew I was going to be out of town. She never considered time zones. She just assumed I'd be back by the time he arrived."

Officer Miller glanced quickly at Flip and continued, "If Social Services agrees it was just a lot of errors on the part of adults, you could have Bobby in, oh, probably three to five days. Unless, of course, they're jammed with cases—and they usually are."

Ronnie spoke up immediately, "Officer, you can't put a little kid through that. He's perfectly fine; Flip was good with him. He was scared when his father didn't show."

Flip was grateful for Ronnie jumping to his defense, but he wished he'd listened to her earlier, or at least planted his fist into Mr. Weber's face for the blonde remark.

The man now looked like someone drained of all body fluids. He slumped in his chair, his face ashen, his jaw slack and drooping, and for the first time, he was speechless.

"What's the other way of handling this?" Flip returned his focus to the two policemen. "I think the boy needs to be with family." Flip couldn't believe his act of kindness had gotten so out of hand.

"Well, the second choice is Mr. Weber could give us a statement for our report that he approved of yours and Miss Talbot's actions and that's about it. Bobby could go home with him right now."

"Officer Barnes," John Weber found his voice. "That's what I think is best. If your partner thinks Bobby is unharmed and I agree, I'd just like to forget the whole thing. May I please see my son?"

"I think that's in order, but first I imagine you'll want to apologize to these good people for your behavior—especially this lovely blonde lady."

"Oh, yes, I do. I'm sorry. I didn't mean to go off the deep end, but it's been a difficult divorce and I just got Helen to agree to let Bobby visit."

He extended his hand to Ronnie. "Miss Talbot, I apolo¬gize for my remark. I was upset. My ex-wife's actually a brunette; she bleaches her hair."

Ronnie hesitated, then shook his hand. "Mr. Weber, you must find other ways to deal with your frustrations. Bobby is a child, not a ping-pong ball or a poker chip." She ended the handshake and stepped back.

"By the way, I'm a natural blonde and I hold degrees in aeronautical engineering and psychology."

Flip hoped Ronnie missed the look of surprise on his face. Until very recently, his opinion of blondes, particularly pretty ones, hadn't differed far from Mr. Weber's. He couldn't imagine she'd be one to hide her intelligence and mentally noted the assumptions he'd made based on his own biases. God, her being so educated could make him feel inadequate if he wasn't careful.

As the officers were leaving with the reunited father and son, burly Officer Miller stopped at the door. "Hey, Captain, none of this report will find its way back to your company. I suppose you'd rather it be that way, wouldn't you?"

"Well, I probably wouldn't have a problem in any case, but First Officer Talbot is new, and it's better if nothing out of the ordinary shows up in her file."

"That's what I figured. By the way, what are the chances of getting a tour on one of those big jets for my boy and nine of his Cub Scout buddies?"

"You mean fly somewhere?" Flip almost swallowed his tongue. Fares were increasing with every hike in fuel prices. For ten kids plus an adult supervisor, round-trip, he calculated to be close to a couple of grand. Gone were the days when airlines could afford the open door policy of years past. All that came to an end with 9/11.

"Oh no, Billy can't fly—gets sick and tosses his cookies. I just meant an on-the-ground tour…maybe when you have a stopover here or something."

"Well, it could be a problem—9/11 pretty much squelched that kind of PR treatment. But give me your card and maybe I can arrange something with the airport manager. The fact that you're law enforcement could be a big plus. Maybe it could be done some evening when the plane's in for maintenance."

Feeling relief that he wasn't going to have to finance a Cub Scout field trip, Flip accepted the officer's card and handed Officer Miller one of his own. "I'll call you if I can set it up. I'll need at least a week or maybe more to clear it with management. Be glad to meet your boy."

He shut the door, closed his eyes and leaned his back against it. "Whew, thank God that's over with. Remind me next time never to bring home any stray kids, dogs, cats or—"

"—women?"

The comment opened Flip's eyes wide. Ronnie's face was just inches from his. She stood on tiptoe and through gritted teeth, she sputtered, "Don't worry. I won't be around the next time to say, 'I told you so.'"

"What's the matter?" Flip had no idea what he'd done to bring on her rage, which resembled a deep-freeze set on fire.

"The matter is you. You arrogant, meddling, lying, overblown, conceited jet jockey. 'Best if nothing out of the ordinary shows up in her file?' Just whose record were you really protecting?" She nailed him to the door, jabbing her finger into his chest, her words slicing through him like a blade through a ripe watermelon.

When Ronnie whirled away, Flip took the advantage and moved to the center of the room, giving her a wide berth as she grabbed her jacket and handbag from the chair.

She started for the door, then spun around again, her blue eyes blazing. "'She's got a way with kids.' Excuse me. Because of you, Mr. Know-It-All, I have been assaulted by a pint-size bully, had catsup splattered all over my uniform, endured insults about my looks and my intelligence, and been accused of kidnapping."

She strode to the door, and not bothering to turn around, yelled, "I have wasted precious hours so you could play rescuer. Now I'm going home to sleep."

She slammed out, sending vibrations through his eardrums that only the roar of a jet engine could equal. He smiled. *What a woman.*

~~~

Flip hit the button opening one side of his two-car garage. Tucking the keys to his Jeep Cherokee in his pocket, he grabbed a soft cotton

T-shirt out of one of the bags he was carrying and dusted off his latest toy: a beautiful black and chrome Harley Davidson. He'd shown it to his dad, Mike, Jack and all his close buddies but hadn't gotten around to breaking the news to Mom yet. He'd have to do that…one of these days.

Stuffing the T-shirt back into the bag of laundry, he crammed it and another bag full of dry cleaning into the back seat of the Cherokee.

He'd done everything he could think of to keep his mind off the icy blonde who'd read him the riot act last night. He still needed to make arrangements to pick up the MG at the airport. He really didn't know why he kept the old classic except that he had a weakness for the extraordinary. But that car always needed parts or repair.

Flip had spent the first part of the morning with aimless chores like checking his computer to make sure his bills had been paid, answering email messages and scanning his investment file. After a stop at the cleaners, he would head for the gym for a vigorous workout.

~~~

Flip undid all his good work at the gym by stopping off at the taco shop on his way home. Now, sprawled on his sofa fighting heartburn from the *carne asada* burrito, Flip chuckled as he listened to Jack explain his latest conquest and catastrophe.

Adjusting the phone to his other ear, Flip gently scolded, "Well, listen, pal: Take care of yourself and stay off the roller blades—or at least next time wear pads."

"Sorry I can't take you to pick up your car, man. I know my accident puts you in a bind, Flip, and I'm bummed, but man, if you could see this chick. I mean, long, black hair clear to her butt, green eyes and a body… Oh, she's so bad."

"Jack, I'll manage." Flip shifted the receiver from one ear to the other. "You just take care of your broken bones." He conjured up a vision of his best friend in a cast from knee to toes and splints on the fingers of both hands.

"Angela said rollerblading was easy to learn." Jack continued, "I'm a jock, right?" Not waiting for Flip's response, Jack gloated, "But there is a bright side to this. I'm on paid sick leave. With sexy Angela bringing me chicken soup and playing chauffeur until the cast comes off, I may never recover."

"I should have known you'd turn this to your advan¬tage." Flip made a few more wise cracks and still chuckling, replaced the phone in its cradle.

Flip fished the leather Global directory out of the small drawer in the end table. Scanning the pages, he made mental notes. Couldn't call Marsha; she was home with sick kids. He wouldn't even think of calling Janet—keeping her out of his hotel room after dinner in Baltimore had turned into an Olympic feat. Of course, there was always family, but they lived so far out of town.

Suddenly a light bulb flashed in Flip's head and get¬ting the car suddenly seemed unimportant. Jack was going to be off the line and someone would have to be assigned to fill his spot.

Grinning from ear to ear, he mused out loud, "Okay now, let's see if I can turn this to *my* advantage as well. Who do I know in scheduling?"

Grabbing the phone again, Flip punched in the familiar number and waited for his call to be answered. His charm could melt the abominable snowman. If he just had time, he could thaw the frosty Ronnie Talbot as well. As soon as the voice came over the line, Flip knew he was living right.

"Donald, my good buddy, Flip Farrell here."

"Okay, Flip, what do you want this time?"

"Donald, you wound me, man. I just called to inquire about your health and to give you a hand with next month's scheduling."

"How many days off do you want to shift? What flights do I have to cover for you? I'm telling you, Flip, getting those Cutting Blade concert tickets was great, but I think I've paid for them by now."

Flip smiled. The father of a fourteen-year-old girl, Donald had been the thrilled recipient of four tickets to the last engagement of the hottest boy band. This generous offering was courtesy of none other than Flip Farrell, childhood friend of Cory Davis, lead singer.

Flip had grown up in the house next door to the Davis family, and in spite of the fact that Cory was only two years younger than Flip, Cory'd become an overnight sensation with the teen scene. A phenomenon Flip couldn't understand until Cory finally clued him in that, according to all his bios, he'd just turned twenty-three. After hitting it big, Cory never failed to give Flip a call when he was in town, pass out free show tickets or send Flip's mother flowers on her birthday.

Aside from the longtime friendship, Flip suspected these were payment for his silence about Cory's real age. At any rate, the tickets had come in handy for improving Flip's schedule or moving around vacation days.

"How can you besmirch my reputation by suggesting that my generous contribution to your child's happiness, not to mention the most glorious birthday of her life, was given with an ulterior motive?"

"Cut the crap, Flip, just name your blackmail."

"Okay," Flip answered after hearing the impatience in Donald's voice, "I actually just wondered if you'd heard about Jack and the roller derby contest he lost. Have you made the replacement yet?" Flip leaned back and propped his feet up on the coffee table. "So who's my copilot? That's all: simple information."

Flip heard Donald's disgusted sigh. "So who do ya want? McGee? Franklin? Who?"

Knowing he may be asking for a month of grief, but unable to help himself, he plunged ahead. "What about Talbot? She's on reserve for a while and I know she could use some time with an experienced captain."

"Well, she'll be getting that. I assigned her to fill a vacation spot for Rhodes. He's blocked with Fuller and that guy's been flying since wings were invented."

"Oh, he's definitely experienced. But did you clear it with his wife?"

"What the hell are you talking about?" Donald shouted. Flip held the phone away from his ear.

"Well, you know he's barely holding his marriage together now and if his wife sees who he's flying with, she'll blow a gasket…which means, of course, he's going to have to call in sick, which is going to leave you with a mess of trips to cover. How many reserve captains do you have on the list?"

"Not enough," Donald grumbled. "Are you sure Fuller's wife is that jealous?"

Flip removed his feet from the table and placed them on the floor. Leaning forward on the couch, he gestured to the empty room with his free hand. "Does she or does she not meet every one of his flights?"

"Isn't that because she really missed him?"

"How many multiple overnights does he do? Aren't most of his trips ball-buster turnarounds with only minimum rest?"

"Well, yeah, he bids the bad trips, but I just figured he was a company man."

"Listen, he's had three marriages already. The child support alone is killing him." Flip could almost see Donald chewing on his pencil while he tried to find an out.

God, I am good.

Flip fought to keep a concerned tone in his voice. "Fuller can't afford another screw-up. You can't put a dish like Talbot in his cockpit, man. It'd be cruel to tempt him."

"Well, I guess I could switch Talbot to your block. About the same hours, better trips. She ought to be glad about that. I could put that other new hire—what's his name?—Jordan, with Fuller. Okay, Flip, it's done. I'll call the people."

"Ah, one more thing, Donald: Don't tell Talbot she's blocked with me for all of next month."

"Why? Am I getting screwed here?"

"Not at all, buddy, ye of little trust. I just want to surprise her. By the end of the month, she'll be rewarding you with fresh-baked peanut butter cookies."

"Yeah, well, for all I do for you, I should get about a bushel of them. Plus, my kid wants to know why Cory Davis hasn't sent her the autographed photo you said he'd send."

"Donald, your kid's wish is my command." Flip broke the connection and swore silently under his breath. Damn Cory. Too bad his nose wasn't broken in too many places to repair when they'd had that last row in junior high. Wonder if he'd still have made it as a teen idol.

~~~

Ronnie stacked the tri-folded towels, carried them to the linen closet and placed them according to size and color. She straightened the row of washcloths and unopened packages of soap and toilet tissue. Satisfied that they were perfectly aligned, she closed the doors and left the hallway.

Picking up her purse and car keys from the table in the entryway, she had her hand on the doorknob when the ringing phone stopped her in her tracks.

It had to be her mother. Who else could it be? She'd returned the accountant's call, and she really didn't know that many people. Sighing, she unzipped her purse and clicked on her cell phone, regretting that she'd given her mother both phone numbers.

"Mother, I don't have time to talk."

"Well, this isn't Mother, but I won't keep you, I promise."

"What do you want?" Ronnie recognized Flip's voice, and while the anger of the previous evening no longer existed, she couldn't explain the little burst of excitement she felt hearing his playful, teasing voice.

"I need a ride to the airport."

"But I'm not going to the airport." She was glad he couldn't see the grin spreading across her face. He wasn't her type, yet she had to admire his perseverance.

"So, where are you going?" His voice literally purred as she listened, knowing full well that she had become a challenge to him.

Okay, he was asking for it. "Well, I was on my way to jog on the beach," she lied, then added, "and afterwards, grocery shopping."

"What a coincidence. I run on the beach, too. What beach?"

She was beginning to dread giving him her phone number as she did with her mother. Was he going to be a pest?

"So, what beach?"

He just doesn't give up and he's lying, she thought. "I run from my condo on Crown Point to La Jolla and back. I'm sorry, but it's not even close to your neighborhood."

"Hey, I love to run—do it all the time. Why don't I meet you?"

"What about getting your car? Why not just run to the airport?" While she hadn't planned on running or making plans with anyone, getting out of the house was definitely a better idea than getting caught there by her mom.

"I'll get the car whenever, and I do have other means of transportation. Give me fifteen minutes and your address."

Against her better judgment, Ronnie found herself rattling off the address of her condo. Whatever was she thinking? He was so typical of every hotshot, gorgeous male she'd ever encountered. She frowned at her image in the small arrangement of mirrors on the wall, then returned to the bathroom to freshen her makeup.

The sound outside her window was deafening. Like a chainsaw on max power, the noise permeated the condo and sent Ronnie running to open the drapes.

Unprepared for the sight of Flip straddling a huge motorcycle, she took in the shiny black helmet with tinted face shield, which gave him the look of a knight in modern-day armor.

Traveling down his broad shoulders, her eyes gave an appraising look to the tight black leather jacket tapering at his trim waistline. She let her gaze slide farther down to the long, lean limbs encased in snug Levis and finally ending at the heavy, sturdy boots. My God, how would she stay strong in a battle of values with this gladiator?

She joined him on the driveway as he removed his gloves, then helmet, raking his fingers through his tousled hair.

"Somehow, I just don't think running is going to work in an outfit like that." She watched as one stubborn tuft fell forward again, causing him to flinch and give it a second brush with the heel of his hand.

"Believe it or not, I've got my running gear in the saddlebags."

"I see you also have another helmet. Do you need a spare in case you crash into a tree?" Ronnie wanted to see if she could undermine his infernal confidence.

"Listen, babe, this little machine isn't any more difficult than maneuvering a B757 or 767. Give me some credit here."

Affixing her brightest smile, Ronnie said, "Well, I'm not sure I dare. If your head gets any bigger, neither helmet will fit."

"Okay, you've made your point."

Flip grinned, then squinted as the sun reflected off the chrome accents of the bike and flashed into his face. Ronnie thought it gave his gray eyes an almost luminous effect. Which, in turn, affected her more than she'd ever imagined.

"Come on, blow off the run and go for a ride with me."

Flip's voice dared her. She started to protest; then the emptiness she'd felt the past few days seemed to engulf her. Would the world really come crashing down if she just once decided to do something foolish and totally irrespon¬sible? It seemed as if she'd spent her entire life doing the expected and proper thing. The high-achieving, polished, perfect lady—and recently, lonelier than even she'd wanted to admit.

"I've always been curious about what it would be like to ride on one of these monsters."

"Here's your chance to find out."

Ronnie brushed a lock of wind-blown hair from her eyes, then trailed her fingers down her face until they rested nervously on her jaw line. She was sure Flip noted her indecision and doubt when he rushed to reassure her.

"Hey, I'm perfectly safe on these things. I took the safety course and everything."

She hadn't once doubted his ability to control the machine; it was the weakening of own resolve that troubled her.

"Where would we go?" Ronnie chewed her bottom lip and jammed her hands into the pockets of her shorts to keep them from fluttering about like a couple of paper kites.

"I'm told the mountains are beautiful about now. It's the only place in the county you'll be able to see and feel real autumn."

She loved it when the leaves turned warm, rich hues of gold, red and rust. The thought of that beauty made up her mind.

"Okay, hotshot, you're on." Indicating her shorts and T-shirt, she said, "Let me go change."

"Now you're talking."

Although he hadn't been invited, Ronnie didn't stop him from following her. Inside, he unzipped his jacket and she watched his eyes sweep about the room. Suddenly feeling ill at ease in his presence, she stammered something and hurried to her bedroom to change her clothes.

What would she wear? She wanted something to withstand the elements and yet she truly had no desire to encourage this man. He was still arrogant, self-possessed and much too confident where women were concerned. She refused to be another one of his conquests.

Holding up a pair of leather pants and matching jacket, she hesitated. The pants fit like a second skin, but they would be perfect for riding a motorcycle and they went with her boots really well. It was the right outfit for the activity, she assured herself. It wasn't like she was *trying* to look sexy.

Chapter 4

A cozy blaze crackled from the stone fireplace in the small, rustic restaurant. The flickering candle on the table cast a glow on Ronnie's face. Flip didn't know when he'd seen anyone as beautiful. In the soft lighting, her hair shimmered, and though she'd run a comb through it, a few strands refused to behave. They brushed her cheeks whenever she lowered her chin.

"See, I always make good on my promises. Do you want another glass of wine?"

She'd been quiet, absentmindedly tracing her fingertips along the rim of the wineglass. Now she lifted her head, eyes wide. "What?" she asked, as if she'd forgotten he was sitting right across from her.

"Where were you just now?" Flip pushed his coffee cup aside and leaned both elbows on the table. He wondered about the secrets that made her so sad. The ones that took her miles away. Did anyone ever break through that facade?

Flushing, she laughed nervously and apologized. "Sorry, I was feeling relaxed—contented. Forgive me. What were you saying?"

Thinking more wine might put her to sleep, Flip glanced out the chintz-curtained window and noted the sun had begun to sink a bit. "Are you tired? Do you want to head back?"

"I suppose we should, but I've enjoyed the day. Thank you so much."

"My pleasure." Flip suddenly couldn't bear to have the day end. He wanted to keep looking at her until he'd memorized all her features. What was going on with him? He'd never had a woman affect him like this. The need to protect her bothered him. Although he was sure if he ever voiced that concern, she'd give him another dressing-down loaded with insults.

While the thought of riding down the mountain after dark was not a real smart idea, he couldn't let go of her yet. Popping in on his parents was the last thing in his mind and yet he found himself saying, "I thought I might stop off and see my folks if you don't mind? They live just around the next bend."

"Your family lives in the mountains? Is that why we came up here?" Flip could tell by her grimace that the idea of a visit did not sit well with her.

Actually it didn't thrill him either. He knew Mom would give him a bad time about the bike; she still treated him like a reckless teen.

He saw Ronnie gathering the courage to protest and God knows he didn't want his folks to get the wrong idea. It wasn't like he was serious about this girl.

Nevertheless, he continued, almost babbling, to convince her. "They moved up here when Dad retired last year. It's been weeks since I've seen either of them, and they aren't getting any younger."

"Well, I'm sure your family would like it if we stopped by. But we can't stay long. It'll be dusk soon." Ronnie didn't protest when he helped her into her jacket, gently freeing her hair as she zipped up the front.

It was all he could do to keep from burying his face and inhaling the wonderful fragrance that came from what he'd describe as gold spun silk.

"It's okay with you then?" He knew he'd backed her into a corner and felt lousy about it, but not lousy enough to retract it.

"As long as we don't stay long. I have things I need to do tonight."

"A quick hello and we'll split," he reassured her. He hoped it was convincing. His mother was always finding ways to extend her children's visits.

He'd counted on Ronnie's good manners; he knew she'd be gracious and agree to his suggestion. After all, he'd been a perfect gentleman all day and how could she fault him for being a dutiful son?

Ronnie gave him a weak smile as he paid the check and escorted her out the door to the Harley.

~~~

Ronnie wrapped her arms around Flip's waist and leaned into him. The mountain road made her heart jump just a bit, and she fought the urge to tighten her hold on Flip. Thank God, he was as competent in controlling this hunk of metal and chrome as he'd led her to believe.

Hearing the motor idle down, it sounded like a chant. *Potato-Potato-Potato.*

The bike came to a complete stop on a flat surface that had changed from blacktop to small gravel. Ronnie opened her eyes and lifted her head to get a better look at her surroundings.

Directly in front of them at the end of the gravel drive was a lodge. Large cedar decks wrapped around the front, supported by huge pillars of rough timber, actually more like the trunks of mature trees. Glass windows reached from the deck to the peak of the steep roof, lending an almost cathedral appearance. Large spruce and cedar clustered across the grassy area in front of the lodge while sprawling oaks stood majestic along the drive. Leaves of gold and red fluttered down, chasing small squirrels out of their paths.

"Where are we?" Ronnie took off her helmet, wondering if she'd been transported back East to rural Connecticut or Vermont. Her face chilled from the brisk breeze; she smelled the fragrance of smoke as it wafted from the wide chimney reaching beyond the roof.

Flip turned off the key, put the stand down, then removed his helmet. "It's Mom and Dad's cabin." Ronnie swung her leg over and planted both feet on the ground; then Flip dismounted.

"My God, it's beautiful. They get to live here all the time?"

Cabin? Ronnie let her gaze travel upward to the tall trees. A finger of the late afternoon sunshine splintered through the branches, blinding her momentarily.

"Yeah, it's nice, huh?" Flip secured both helmets to the bike. Removing his gloves, he stuffed them into his jacket pocket. Flip took Ronnie's slightly chilled hand in his warm one. It felt good.

Ronnie matched her stride with Flip's as they walked up the path to the wide stairs that led to the deck. The door suddenly opened and a handsome man with a strong resemblance to Flip bolted onto the deck.

"As I live and breathe, it's my baby brother."

"Mike. What cat dragged you in, man?"

Flip dropped Ronnie's hand in time to catch the bulk throwing himself in Flip's direction. Ronnie watched with total amazement and fascination as both men began to plummet and pound one another with short, quick jabs to biceps and bellies.

"All right already, you overgrown delinquents. Knock it off. I think we have company."

Ronnie lifted her gaze from the wrestling duo to a tall silver-haired man standing at the rail in a pair of faded Levi's and flannel shirt. His chin bore a cleft identical to ones on the two younger men still playfully exchanging insults and punches.

"Flip, Mike, have you two totally forgotten your manners?" He descended the stairs and approached Ronnie, grinning broadly. "Does this lovely young lady have a name?" Taking her hand in his, he introduced himself and gave a pseudo-frown to the younger men.

"Mr. Farrell, so nice to meet you. I'm Ronnie Talbot. Or should I call you Captain?" Ronnie returned the handshake and glanced at Mike and Flip, still grappling and acting like twelve-year-olds.

"Ronnie, my pleasure. Please, call me Ken. I'm afraid Captain Farrell could be a bit confusing since we might all answer."

"Mike," Ken said, nodding at the dueling duo, who immediately stopped the horseplay and were attempting to regain some degree of civility, "flies for Freight Express."

"They don't trust him hauling people," Flip remarked, then dodged as Mike feigned another punch to Flip's mid-section. Flip smoothed back his hair, draped his arm across Mike's shoulder and faced her. "As usual, my dad succeeds in making me look bad, when it's plain to see that it's this derelict's fault." He jabbed a thumb in Mike's shoulder.

"So you've met Dad, and this sorry creature is my brother, Mike." He gave Mike a smirk. "Ronnie flies right seat. Eat your heart out."

Mike moved beyond his brother's reach and took both Ronnie's hands in his. "Ronnie? It's a pleasure. But I have to warn you that we met just in the nick of time."

Perplexed and slightly embarrassed at the rowdiness she'd witnessed, Ronnie looked at the Flip before she answered Mike. "Why is that?"

"Good Lord, woman, I can save you from this ugly specimen of manhood, not to mention his total lack of personality."

"Okay, you two, don't destroy the family name and honor before she gets to meet the best part of all of us."

Ronnie found herself being ushered into the house by the tall trio of good-looking men. She'd no sooner stepped inside than the scent of cinnamon and something she couldn't describe filled her nostrils.

Flip sniffed the air and yelled to no one in particular, "Mom's cinnamon rolls." Deserting the group, he quickly crossed the polished hardwood floor toward the kitchen. He turned back to her and said, "Come on, Ronnie, you gotta have one of my mom's rolls."

"Excuse me? Did I hear a *please*?" Between the kitchen area and the giant fireplace, which commanded full attention of the main room, a woman came down the stairs holding a puppy in her arms. Her dark hair was streaked with silver around her face and her eyes sparkled as she did her best to fight the smile that showed the deep dimples in her cheeks.

Ken met her at the bottom of the stairs and said, "Honey, our worst nightmare has come true: The twins are home at the same time." He scooped the puppy out of her arms and motioned Ronnie closer. "Ronnie, I want you to meet Ginny, mother of those two thugs in the kitchen, and the beauty and the brains of the family. Honey, this is Ronnie Talbot. She flies with Flip."

Ronnie stepped forward, extended her hand and with the other, scratched the puppy's head. "Mrs. Farrell, so nice to meet you." She could see immediately where Flip got his gray eyes. His mother's were the same shade, but took on an almost amethyst tint, reflecting the shade of her knitted shirt.

Ronnie looked at the two younger men huddled in the kitchen over a warm pan of cinnamon rolls. "I can see that Flip and Mike look alike, but I didn't know they were twins. Mike called him his baby brother."

"I know. Mike's fifteen minutes older and they're so competitive, they argue about everything. Ronnie? What an unusual name for a girl? Is it short for Veronica? Or did your dad want a boy?"

"Yes, Veronica… Ah, I don't know." Ronnie stammered, silently chiding herself for sounding so flustered and stupid. "I guess I never asked." But how could she ask her father if he'd wanted a boy when she never even met the man?

She was grateful for Flip's interruption as he joined the group and planted a big kiss on his mother's cheek. "Hi, Mom. You were expecting me. You made rolls."

Ginny massaged her face and with a pained expression groaned, "Aw, Flip, you've got sticky all over me. Those rolls were for breakfast and how could I have known you were coming? You never call, you never—"

"—write." Flip finished her sentence as he wrapped both arms around his mother in a huge bear hug. "I know. I'm a bad boy."

Watching mother and son experience the joy of just being together, Ronnie felt a lump form in her throat. The love between them was obvious. She turned away, ashamed that she was so envious. Afraid she would not be able to control the hint of tears lurking in the corners of her eyes, she focused on the piano near floor-to-ceiling windows adjacent to the huge fireplace.

"Oh, you have a piano." Ronnie approached the baby grand. A small display of family photos in silver frames adorned the top.

"Do you play?" Ginny joined her and pulled out the bench.

"Oh, not really. I used to, but it's been ages." She wanted to bolt and run. This was unexpected and she knew she wasn't succeeding in hiding her uneasiness. Seeing the piano brought back memories she'd tried to shove out of her mind. Not so much playing the instrument—she'd loved making the keys come alive. It was just that she had to have a talent to win contests. It was a miracle she didn't hate pianos with the pressure her mother had put on her to be the best. She felt Flip's gaze, but didn't return it.

"Please, try it. It's like riding a bike." Ginny sat down and patted the bench beside her.

"You first, Mrs. Farrell." Ronnie was aching to let her fingers touch the keys, but she couldn't quite trust herself just yet. They were sure to tremble, she thought. But wouldn't it be fun to play just

once for pleasure? Not to practice or compete or impress anyone—
just to enjoy the music.

"I'll go first, on one condition." Ginny's eyes twinkled and her
dimples deepened. Leaning closer to Ronnie, she whispered, "Quit
calling me Mrs. Farrell. I keep looking around for Ken's mother."

Ronnie nodded her agreement and let Ginny's playing envelop
her as she relaxed and listened. Ginny played a medley of everything
from classical to pop, finishing with a boogie-woogie tune that put
all three males into various gyrations of movement.

"Now it's your turn." Ginny said above the din created by
applause and cheering and the dog's howling.

"Well, I'll try, but I've forgotten so much." Ronnie nervously
rested her fingers on the ivory keys and began one of her favorite
pieces. It was one she'd practiced thousands of times before, her
standard talent contribution at every beauty pageant she'd ever
entered: Mozart's Concerto no. 20 in D Minor.

Ronnie closed her eyes and lost herself in the music. Her fingers
flew over the keys and the melody filled her soul with joy, as it
always had. Reality slipped away and Ronnie soared. It was much
like the feeling she got sitting behind the controls of a plane. Her
touch made each instrument perform. Like controlling a flying
monster, to make music she had to be perfect. A grin spilled across
her face as she thought of the roar of a jet engine and a piano melody
both as music.

~~~

Flip was mesmerized. This was a side of Ronnie he'd never
imagined. She didn't stumble or hesitate, just raced up and down the
keys as if she were onstage at a concert hall.

Happiness radiated from her face, and for some reason, it pleased
him. He'd seen the confidence she'd shown in the cockpit, but this
wasn't technical knowledge one gleaned out of books or ground

school. This was a talent, God-given and, as far as he could tell, flawless.

The piano was quiet. For a few minutes, no one spoke; then Flip moved closer to the bench and placed his hand lightly on Ronnie's shoulder.

"Ronnie, that was beautiful. How long have you been playing?" Flip asked.

Ken and Mike added their praise with hearty applause and enthusiastic "Bravos."

"My dear, Flip is right," Ginny exclaimed. "That was wonderful. Your talent is far from ordinary. You must have studied extensively."

Flip watched Ronnie lapse into the discomfort she'd shown earlier. Her face flushed and in place of a smile, she bit her lower lip.

"Oh, you're just being nice. I'm so rusty. It was a part of my life for a long time, but not anymore."

"But Ronnie—"

Noting Ronnie's increased agitation, Flip broke in, "Mother, Ronnie and I need to get going."

"What? Oh, of course."

"Flip?" Ken put the puppy on the floor and studied his son for a moment. "You two going to be okay on that metal monster out there? The wind is pretty chilly. I wouldn't be surprised if we didn't get a frost tonight."

Mike walked over to the window and peered out into the darkness. "Bro, are you sure you want to take that thing down the mountain at night?"

"Whatever are you two talking about?" Ginny looked from Ken to Mike, then drilled Flip with a gaze like steel cutting through butter.

"What *metal monster*? What *thing*? Trenton Maxwell Farrell, what are you hiding?"

The jig was up. Flip decided to just dummy up; he'd attempt to sneak away without having to listen to her you're-going-to-break-your-neck speech. God knows he could recite it chapter and verse.

"Mom, it's nothing. I'll call you tomorrow. Ronnie, get your jacket."

Ginny slid off the bench and marched to the front door. The puppy must have thought he was being taken for a walk outside since he began to yap and dance back and forth.

"Uh-oh. You're nailed, bro."

"Flip, didn't you mention it to your mom?" Flip shook his head at his dad's inquiry.

"What's the matter?" Ronnie asked.

Flip could see she was totally confused by their behavior.

Ginny's shriek was loud enough to pierce an eardrum. "I can't believe you bought another motorcycle!"

Ginny whirled around; her gray eyes sent daggers at Flip, but since it was obvious the other men had known about it, they didn't escape her glare.

"Mom, I know you don't like them, but I'm not sixteen and I know how to ride. We'll be safe."

Ken whispered to Ronnie, "Flip and Mike bought a bike when they were sixteen and didn't tell her."

"Yeah," Mike chimed in, "we could have convinced her to let us keep it if the idiot hadn't done a wheelie and almost killed himself. Wrecked the bike, too, and I'd only ridden it once."

Flip knew he could just leave and Mom would eventually get over her mad spell. But he also knew that when he'd lain in that hospital for five days in a coma, it had been more than just her being mad about the bike—she'd thought he was going to die.

He crossed to the door and put his arm around Ginny. "Mom, I'm all grown up. I took a safety course and I don't take chances. Do you honestly think I would risk Ronnie if I weren't sure I could handle it? I'm safe, really."

He watched Ginny dab at her eyes, and then, with a sternness that was familiar to him, she said, "Well, the least you can do is stay over until morning."

"Mom, I can't do that." He wasn't about to waffle and obey like a ten-year-old. How would that look to Ronnie?

"Nonsense. We have plenty of room. You can bunk with Mike in the den, and Ronnie can have the guest room."

"Mom, I told you—" It suddenly occurred to Flip that even though this was not how he'd have chosen to spend his first night with Ronnie, it did put them under the same roof. "Is there nothing I can do or say to change your mind?"

He turned to Ronnie, shrugged and held his hands, palms up, in a helpless gesture. "Ronnie, I'm sorry but I've learned there's no point in arguing with this woman when she puts her tiny foot down."

He watched Ronnie's expression cloud over, and for a moment, considered overriding his mom's orders. It was too late.

Ginny retraced her steps, ushering Ronnie toward the staircase. "Come on, Ronnie. I'll show you the room and then we'll see about dinner."

"Mrs. Farr—er, Ginny, I can't stay. I don't even have a toothbrush." Ronnie continued to protest, but Flip knew it would be to no avail as he watched the two women ascend the stairs.

"Don't worry. In the flying business, you learn to keep spares of every necessity. I never knew when Ken or the boys might bring someone home. I have a whole supply of emergency ditty bags for overnight guests." Ginny's voice faded as she herded Ronnie up the last of the stairs.

"Well, Dad," Mike said, draping an arm across his dad's shoulder, "I think we saw history being made tonight. Flip let Mom win an argument."

"Michael, I believe you might have something there."

Flip looked at the two men and, though he knew they'd seen right through him, felt honor-bound to dispute them vigorously. "Come on. Give me a break. I don't think Ronnie was real thrilled about going down the hill in the dark. That's why I gave in—to spare her any anguish."

"Yeah, right." Mike threw a half-hearted punch to Flip's arm and continued, "Ronnie would rather have gone down in an open chariot pulled by wild horses than stay over."

"Son, I have to agree with Mike. Ronnie looked trapped when your mother took charge." Ken followed Flip and Mike into the living room. The twins settled themselves on the sofa and Ken sat in his leather recliner.

Flip met his father's gaze, "I know. I almost changed my mind, but Mom turned on her usual bulldozer mode."

Flip was beginning to wonder about Ronnie's frosty demeanor. Was she just trying to hide fear? There was something vulnerable Flip couldn't quite identify. He did, however, recognize a need in himself to protect her—and that also puzzled him.

"Ronnie looked almost scared. What's going on with her? Is she this insecure in the cockpit?"

"No. That's the weird thing. In the aircraft, she's as confident and competent as she was at the piano tonight. She's quiet with people, but scared? No, she's on top of everything at work. It's like she's two people."

Mike stretched out and tossed a pillow under his head. "Well, one thing's certain: If she can fly like she plays, we better start looking for a lot of pink sky."

Chapter 5

Flip sat at the breakfast bar next to Mike and watched his dad turn bacon in a skillet. Lifting his mug from the granite countertop, he sipped his coffee and, looking up, caught his father's stare. "What?"

"You know, son, you could have borrowed one of our cars to drive home last night. I was about to offer when you just gave up."

"Are you serious? Dad, Mom would have had her can opener going full speed if I'd left my hog unprotected."

"Your what? Come on, Flip. It's not like the Hell's Angels made you a member of their club or anything." Mike smirked, got off his perch and poured himself another cup of coffee.

"Well, that's what the big boys call 'em." Flip answered good-humoredly and grinned at his brother.

"Hey, Dad, are you doing your famous omelets this morning?"

"That depends on whether you show me how to update my computer or not."

"Okay, okay, I'll walk you through it, but I've got to buzz out right after lunch. I'm picking up a trip to South America and back that's going to pay for my new golf clubs."

"I didn't say anything about including lunch," Ken quipped. "But do you really think new clubs will improve your game?"

Flip enjoyed the banter Mike carried on with their father. In the early years, Ken had been flying on a lot of special occasions, and yet they always managed to hold the family intact.

Christmas sometimes could be three days early or a day late, depending on flight schedules, weather or mechanical breakdowns, but it was always special.

He got the distinct feeling Ronnie had never experi¬enced a feeling of family like he'd grown up with. Fighting the urge to peek in the guestroom, he let his gaze travel to the stairs. "Isn't Mom up yet?" He glanced at his watch and frowned. He'd never known his mother to sleep in this late.

"Oh, she's been up for a while. I think they went out for a walk." Ken whipped the eggs in the bowl and slapped Mike's hand as he tried to sneak a fresh mushroom from the chopping board.

"*They?* You mean Ronnie went too?"

Ken nodded and put Mike to work chopping onions while he drained the bacon between layers of paper towels.

"Since I retired, your mom took up walking every morning. I think it was a sneaky way of getting me to cook. But what the hell—she did it enough years and I kind of like it. Plus, I am really, really good at it."

"Dad, have you ever made a spinach quiche?" Mike was also a fledgling gourmet.

Flip listened to the two men exchanging cooking tips like two chefs. Quiche? My God, wasn't that the thing real men didn't eat, let alone cook? His culinary talents had never advanced past the drive-through or nuke-it level.

He let his mind drift to Ronnie and his mother walking—and what? Talking? What would his mother tell her? He wasn't sure he was comfortable with that whole concept. He had an image to uphold and he could just see his mother pulling out the baby pictures if he didn't get Ronnie out of there soon.

~~~

The back door opened and the two women entered the kitchen. "Mmm. Something smells good." Ginny sniffed appreciatively as she stepped inside the kitchen with Ronnie close behind. Both women had rosy cheeks and tousled hair. Ronnie didn't miss the approving look Flip directed at her.

"I can't believe what's happened. Someone turned our dad into a Mr. Mom—he cooks now." Flip winked at Ronnie as he teased his mother.

"Oh, hush, he likes it." Ginny whipped off her scarf and draped it over Flip's head as she proceeded to the refrigerator.

Ronnie sat down on a barstool next to Flip. He casually placed a hand on her back and gently began to stroke in small circular motions. She didn't object. For the first time in ages, the tightness was gone, and she realized she was totally at ease. She closed her eyes.

As the warmth spread down to her center, she almost ached with desire. Wanting his hand to go lower, exploring…her body, almost drifting…

"Whoa, take it easy." Flip grabbed her just as she almost slipped off the barstool. "Did you fall asleep for a minute there?"

Ronnie sat up abruptly. Now the warmth was in her face and she could only hope it wasn't as red as she suspected it might be. "Sorry, guess I just relaxed a bit too much."

Trying to find a safer subject, she focused on Ginny rummaging through the refrigerator.

"Would you look at this?" Ginny pulled out a small Ziploc bag of cinnamon rolls and held them up for Ronnie to see. "Out of twenty-four rolls, there are exactly three left. Ronnie, would you like one? I can zap it."

"No, thank you, but I'll have a cup of tea if you have any."

"Oh, we have everything. Ginny shops at the supermarket as well as she does at boutiques, and believe me, if it exists, we more than likely have it." Ken reached into a cabinet and pulled out a metal tin and popped the lid off. Setting it in front of Ronnie, he turned on a small spigot at the center island sink and filled the stain¬less steel teapot with water.

Flip pulled an herbal teabag out of the supply with two fingers. "It's probably not quite what you're used to, but it might be close."

Ronnie hoped that wasn't a dig. She detected no edge of sarcasm, and having been a past victim of his sharp tongue, she was aware he could deliver it if he felt so inclined.

Several minutes passed with small talk; then Ken placed a huge plate filled with three strips of bacon, an enormous omelet and two biscuits in front of Ronnie. He plopped two more plates with even more generous servings down for his sons and followed up with glasses of orange juice for everyone.

Ken took two small luncheon plates from a stack and split the final omelet between himself and Ginny. Grinning at Ronnie, he said, "We old codgers have to watch the cholesterol." After Ken served Ronnie a mug of hot water from the teapot, he and Ginny joined the trio at one end of the bar.

Ronnie heard silverware clinking like a background accent to the roar she felt in her head. If her mother ever even suspected she'd gotten this close to this kind of food, she'd have had a fit. It had been so long since she'd actually eaten bacon, she could only vaguely recall its taste.

The aroma was almost overwhelming. She remembered putting it between slices of buttered toast when she was little, but then suddenly, like desserts, fried foods and anything that could be buttered had disappeared from her meals.

Tentatively, she picked up one crisp piece and nibbled at it. She sensed Flip was watching her. She decided to ignore him. Concentrating on the bacon at that moment was probably safer. The taste and the enjoyment of the meal were worth any price.

~~~

The ride down the mountain took less time than she'd originally thought. So why the big fuss about staying over the night before? However, she was glad she'd been forced into it, even if she would never admit it to Flip.

Pulling into the driveway, Flip idled the Harley down, then stopped and turned off the key. Dropping the kickstand, they removed their helmets and Ronnie gingerly got off the bike. The long walk with Ginny that morning had loosened her up a bit, and she wasn't as sore as she'd been the day before.

"Well, thanks for the short ride to the mountains that took two days," she quipped.

"Hey, I'm really sorry about that, but when I was younger I had a bike accident and Mom—"

"—I know," she interrupted. "Mike already told me you wrecked his half of the bike. You have a nice family. I like them."

Flip chuckled. "Yeah, they're cool." He squinted at her as the mid-morning sunshine streaked his face. "You surprise me, Talbot. You're a very complex woman."

"Not like your usual blonde bimbo, eh?"

"Who have you been listening to? I know you've heard I date a lot and I'll accept the fact that some of them were not rocket scientists, but *bimbo* is over the top, just a tad."

Ronnie slipped out of her leather jacket as the day was already heating up, even if the ride down had been brisk. She shouldn't be standing here lollygagging over this hunk like some teenager. Had she lost her grip on total control? Still, she lingered. "So how am I complex?"

Flip let his gaze travel from her incredible blue eyes down to the snug knitted shirt. It showcased her bountiful breasts in perfect alignment with her nipples at attention.

He hoped that effect was a result of his lingering glance. "Well, you're in an industry that doesn't see many women pilots with looks like yours. You are equally at home in the cockpit, er, flight deck, as you are at a piano."

Flip watched her face cloud with uneasiness. Biting her lower lip, she looked away.

"You seem driven to be the best, and to do that, you chill everyone out. But, Ronnie, I see a chink in the glacier every now and then. What keeps you on ice?"

He wasn't prepared when she whirled around, her curt voice lashing out, followed by fury that ignited her eyes.

"You know, if I wanted to see a therapist, I'm capable of picking one. I don't need you or anyone else to pick my personality apart. I'm happy just as I am, and if I do ever decide to seek counseling, you can bet it won't be on your couch."

She shoved the spare helmet at him, spun on her heel and raced toward her front door.

This was getting to be a pattern. He'd thought he was making progress only to end up speechless after she'd ripped him apart once again. Why didn't he learn just to keep his mouth shut? Good God, what would she do if she found out he'd manipulated the schedule?

He jammed his helmet on, secured the spare one and turned the key. Revving up the motor, he gave one quick glance toward the condo before pulling out of the drive. He had to get home and call Donald. He'd have to swear him to secrecy or he'd end up toast. What could he use as payola for Donald's silence?

~~~

Ronnie tossed her jacket on the sofa and grimaced as the phone went tumbling to the floor. He thought she was perfect? She couldn't even remember to keep her phone on the base. She'd have laughed if she weren't so close to tears. She'd lost control. She was having a meltdown. He couldn't see it, but he was responsible.

She plopped on the sofa and pulled her legs up under her chin. She didn't even bother taking off her boots. Resting her cheek on her knees, she wiped at the tear trickling onto her pants. Even with his teasing and his attitude, she sensed he cared. Something she hadn't gotten from a lot of the men in her life.

She hardly knew him. How is it he seemed to know her better than anyone—even her mother?

What am I saying? Mom doesn't know me at all.

For that matter, did Ronnie recognize herself? Questions bounced inside her brain and she had no answers for any of them.

Several minutes passed before Ronnie forced herself off the sofa. She crossed the room and returned the handset to the base. Seeing the blinking red light on her answering machine, she hit the button and the messages began to play.

The first one was her mother. Ronnie listened and she couldn't help comparing the voice on the machine with that of Ginny Farrell.

"Veronica, where in the world are you? I've been trying to reach you for weeks. If you don't return my call, I swear I'm going to have the police check your house. For all I know, you could be lying dead right now. Anyway, I wanted to know if you've sent in that latest application I mailed you. It's for Miss—"

Fortunately, the beep cut her mother off before the message was completed. But the second one succeeded in making Ronnie scream. "Mother, get it through your head! I don't want to be Miss Career 2014 or Miss Grapefruit or Miss anything!"

Hitting the delete button, she wiped out the finishing sentences of her mother's second message.

She listened to the others, but only one caught her interest. She quickly copied the changes scheduling had made in her status. It seemed, instead of being on day-to-day reserve, she'd be flying a block for someone who was either sick or on vacation.

"Well, hallelujah, no more guessing where I'm flying for a whole month."

Ronnie picked up the phone and punched in the number for scheduling. Running her fingers through her wind-tossed hair, she was anxious to jump in the shower. "An assigned block. This is so great," she said as she waited for the line to pick up. Twisting the ends of her hair, she bit her lower lip and waited for someone to answer her call. Thinking about the luxury of not being on a ninety-minute alert had pulled her from the edge of depression almost into euphoria.

"Scheduling, Donald speaking."

"Hi, this is First Officer Talbot. You left a message for me?"

"Ah, yeah, I did. We—we've got you replacing someone who was in an accident. It'll be all month…okay? Gotta go."

"Wait a minute." Ronnie couldn't believe he hadn't even bothered to confirm the block number. She liked being absolutely sure she'd heard the number correctly on her message machine. Besides, she'd like to know with whom she was flying.

Begrudgingly, the scheduler confirmed the number, but when she asked who her captain would be, he disconnected the call. Ronnie looked at the receiver, stuck out her tongue and slammed the phone down in the cradle. "Well, so much for being courteous, Donald whatever-your-last-name-is Rudeness."

Her brows knitted into a frown, but only for a moment. "I'm not going to let him get to me. I have a block and that's all that matters."

Humming to herself, Ronnie went down the hall to shower, kicking off her boots and shedding her shirt as she went. When she reached the bathroom, she realized she'd left a trail of clothing. Noting her unusual behavior, she couldn't suppress a giggle. Shrugging, she thought the world would not end just because Veronica Talbot didn't immediately put her clothes in their proper place. She'd pick them up after her shower.

~~~

For lack of anything better to do, Flip hit the television remote, hoping to catch the midday news. He ambled into his kitchen and poked his head into the refrigerator. He had a beer and a piece of leftover pizza in hand when the phone stopped him from foraging farther into the depths of his Kenmore.

Donald's voice whined, "All right, Flip, you owe me big time. I didn't rat on you, but if she finds out, I could be in big trouble."

Evidently, Ronnie knew she was on a block, but not whose block. Donald sounded paranoid. There was no way she would find out that he'd manipulated the deal if Donald kept his mouth shut.

"Trust me, Donald. She's not going to find out. Relax. You're in the clear."

Flip hung up the phone and rolled his eyes. *This is getting way too complicated. I got to old Donald just in the nick of time; otherwise he'd have blabbed to Ronnie that I requested her to fill Jack's slot.*

Considering how things had been when they'd parted this morning, Flip wasn't sure he'd done himself any favors where Ronnie was concerned.

He could tell Mom liked her. The fact that Ronnie played the piano so well was a big plus in his mom's eyes. She'd nagged all three kids to take lessons, and only his sister, Gloria, had stuck with it. But Gloria's skills were mediocre when compared to Ronnie's.

He wondered why, with talent like that, he hadn't seen a piano in her condo. "Maybe she has a keyboard in another room," he said aloud. "But God, you'd think she'd have a baby grand."

He downed his beer and still clutching the bottle, leaned against the tile counter. He couldn't get her off his mind. She'd looked so cute when she'd come back from the early morning walk with his mom. Her windblown hair, her rosy pink cheeks and her smile. Her smiles were infrequent, but when she did smile, it seemed to Flip that the room got brighter. Unable to keep himself from grinning, he let his thoughts drift back to breakfast. She'd been so relaxed, really enjoyed her food. It was a wonder to Flip how she managed to stay so slim.

"Speaking of which, I won't look too hot if I keep guzzling beer. I better go buy some real food." He set the bottle in the sink and opened the refrigerator to take another inventory of what he needed from the grocery store.

~~~

It had taken Ronnie the entire afternoon to finish the errands she'd abandoned yesterday for the wild ride to the mountains. After a really Spartan dinner, she made herself a cup of herbal tea. Squaring her shoulders and taking a deep breath, she returned her mother's calls.

She was getting to be a polished liar. So good, she herself almost believed what she was saying. "Mom, I know you're disappointed, but I just didn't get the application for that pageant." Twirling her hair, she let her eyes drift to the stack of mail sitting on the hall table. Quickly averting her eyes from one envelope sticking out of the pile, she said, "I've had a lot of trouble with my mail service lately."

Well, technically, she had. Most of it was junk mail, especially the ones from her mother with applications to enter more pageants. In a little while she'd go through it all, piece by piece, and that particular missive would go into the round file.

"You know, Veronica, you aren't getting any younger. Even if we shave four or five years off your birth date, you don't have that much time left to compete."

"Well, it's probably for the best. I haven't been able to practice for ages."

"You said you're making good money. Haven't you bought yourself another piano?" Ronnie could hear the agitation in her mother's voice.

She used to think her mother was on her side. When Ronnie was a preteen, she'd thought pageants were for real, a way to accomplish goals. Mom said they were the stepping stones to a career—a career *Mom* desperately wanted but never managed to achieve for herself.

Then at twenty-one, Ronnie entered Miss Galaxy. The prize money was in the thousands and would've paid for all the flying time she'd need to get her pilot's license. Everyone had told her she had the talent portion sewed up. It was worth fifty percent of the score and she'd never played so perfectly.

She'd actually been shocked when she'd found out she would win only if she slept with the head judge. She hadn't believed him. But Miss New Jersey, whose talent was baton twirling, had won the crown and the money. Later Ronnie had seen the "winner" leaving the theater on the arm of the judge.

"Veronica." Her mother's voice brought her back from her memories. "I don't understand why you want to risk your life flying those—those—airplanes. Do you have any idea what that air does to your skin?" The tone was just a notch below shrieking level.

Even though Ronnie knew it was hopeless, she'd try one more time to explain how much she loved her job.

"Mother, what did I play with when I was little? Toy airplanes, right? How did I break my arm? Remember? Joey Brewster and I built a plane out of orange crates and I crashed jumping off the wall in his backyard."

"You were a kid then, Veronica. You're a beautiful woman now. Use it. For God's sake, do something with what you have. You could be in movies or a model or, at the very least, married to someone who could support you well."

Ronnie shook her head. Her mother would never understand. Ronnie wasn't even sure she did. All she knew was that from the time she was little, the idea of flying was just pure magic. She wasn't going to let anything stand in her way—and she sure as hell wouldn't sell her body to accomplish it.

Only her piano.

She'd sold the piano for flight training. Her scholarships had run out and she had to have a lot of expensive hours in complicated aircraft to get the certificates she'd needed. It was the hardest thing she'd ever done, but when she got seniority, she'd buy another piano.

"Oh, Mom, I've got to hang up. Someone's at my door," Ronnie lied. Making kiss-kiss noises over her mother's objections, she punched the "end call" button and tossed the phone onto the chair.

Tomorrow would be better. She was going to work at a job she loved. She just hoped she didn't get a bad-tempered captain or one on the make.

But her mother was right about one thing: One of these days she was going to have to do something about getting a life that included something other than work. All work and no play—no matter how much she loved her job—was not quite how she planned to live.

Someday she wanted a home, kids and a husband who loved her. Would love her even if she got a wart on her nose, had to wear glasses thick as Coke bottles or had one leg shorter than the other.

After trying the dating scene and ending up with wrestling matches, and guys with more baggage than could be stowed in the cargo section of a 747, she'd become a born-again virgin. God, she wished there was just one decent guy out there who wasn't married, gay—or what? That was as far as she'd ever gotten. If they were decent, most of them were already taken.

Unless…could Trenton Maxwell Farrell aka Captain Flip be that guy? His family sure was nice. She wondered how Flip's mom and dad had survived the airline scenario. It wasn't an industry that inspired strong relationships.

The brutal truth remained: For all her intelligence and for all she'd accomplished, she was still alone. Only in the safe confines of her own condo could she admit to herself how lonely she really was.

Chapter 6

Ronnie glanced in Flip's direction as she acknowledged landing instructions from the tower. Flip returned her gaze, smiled and repeated the checklist items back to her.

She'd endured the awkwardness of that first day. The excitement of having a regular schedule for a whole month had taken over. They were finishing their sixth flight together and thirteen days of the block had passed.

Outside the job, there had been no other contact between them. No motorcycle trips or dinners for two. On duty, it had almost seemed as if Flip wanted to avoid her as much as she wanted to do the same. She was embarrassed at the way she'd acted after the visit to the mountains. It had been one of the nicest times she'd ever had and his family was great. And he was—what? She almost thought he acted guilty, but he didn't pick the crews, scheduling did.

Ronnie still couldn't believe she hadn't checked beforehand to see that Flip was the captain. It was awkward in the beginning. Now she'd recovered from her shock and as they established a routine, things had progressed well. Better than she'd expected.

Ronnie made the last cabin announcement, then willed herself to concentrate on the most crucial steps of the landing. Setting the flaps, Ronnie finished the checklist and the big jet settled, then rolled down the runway at Logan International. The thrusters were activated and the plane slowed gradually until it taxied toward the gate.

"We've got a twenty-four-hour layover. Right now all I want to do is eat and hit the sack." Flip yawned and stretched, and Ronnie tried not to notice how the front of his shirt tightened.

Watching him roll down his sleeves and button the cuffs, she wondered what it would feel like to snuggle close to that broad chest and have those muscled arms folded around her body. Should she inquire if his dinner plans included anyone?

The door opened and Marsha stuck her head inside. "Hey, the crew wants to go have seafood and beer. You guys up for it?"

"Sounds great. You buying?" Flip gave Marsha the thumbs-up salute.

"Oh, right, like I'm Miss Got Rocks. Obviously, you've never bought shoes every six weeks for growing boys. Did I tell you Davy is almost as tall as Benjamin? By the way, both of them want to know when you're coming over to build that tree house like you promised."

Flip grimaced. "Yikes, they never forget anything, do they? Tell them Uncle Flip says soon."

Turning to Ronnie, Flip asked, "What do ya think, Ronnie: How does lobster and steamers sound to you?"

"Sure." Ronnie could barely contain her pleasure at being included in the group. Since she'd been blocked with Flip, she hadn't spent one lonely night in the hotel room like she used to. "I'm up for it," she said.

Flip was always included, or more to the point, the group revolved around him. He was fun. The guys got along with him and the girls flirted with him, even the married ones. But Ronnie had noticed he never crossed the line. He had a good time, but the reputation she'd been warned about seemed to have been fabricated—or else Flip had changed a lot.

~~~

After checking into the hotel and changing into casual wear, the whole crew piled into cabs in search of seafood at the famous Blarney's Pub.

In the wintertime, the quaint pub was a favorite with airline crews and locals alike because the ice rink was right across the street. People met for dinner, then skated off the calories on the ice. The lobster and steamers were delicious and the clam chowder was to die for. Pitchers of beer disappeared at an alarming rate.

"Marsha, I don't even drink," Ronnie tittered as she tried to ignore the beer refill Marsha poured her. "I only drink one little, tiny glass of wine on very special occasions."

Ronnie picked up the shot of whiskey Stan, the male flight attendant, had ordered and downed it in one gulp. Blinking, she caught Flip's gaze, and for some reason the surprised look on his face amused her. She began to giggle uncontrollably.

"Well, for someone who doesn't drink, you sure know a neat trick because this is the third time I've filled you up." Marsha chortled and plopped back in her seat. The beer sloshed over the side of the pitcher and began to run in small rivulets across the Formica tabletop.

"Hey, kids," Flip said, hastily mopping the spill with his napkin, "it's nearly eight hours until check-in tomorrow. It's time to cut you off. Anyway, I think we all could do with a bit of fresh air. Let's walk around a bit."

"Are you nuts, Frip? It fleezing out there." Marsha's slurred words sent Ronnie into a fit of giggling snorts and hiccups.

Flip slipped his arm around Ronnie and pulled her out of the booth while another flight attendant struggled to get Marsha into an upright position. "I told her she shouldn't drink anything when she diets. She's hasn't eaten anything all day."

Marsha swayed, brushed off her friend and squared her shoulders. Indignantly, she protested, "It's not the diet, Barbara. It's just hot in here. Frip's right—we need fresh air. Come on, Ronnie, let's go ice-skating."

Flip's attempts to stop the giggling blonde and her chubby companion were in vain. He threw money on the table while Barbara, Stan and the other flight attendant grabbed the jackets, scarves and gloves that Ronnie and Marsha left in the booth.

"Skates for everybody," Ronnie announced and pulled a wad of money out of her wallet. Flip grabbed her arm and restrained her from waving the bills around her head, as several onlookers appeared as if they might take her up on the offer.

"I'm a good skater. Did you know that? I'm as good as Nancy Kerrigan, Flip-p." Ronnie leaned close when she pronounced the p in his nickname.

Flip realized she couldn't have passed a Breathalyzer test from ten paces back.

"I took lessons for a long, long time but then M-Mom said it wasn't a good talent for Miss Floooridaa. We lived there for a while too."

Ronnie swayed against Flip and then, grinning from ear to ear, she stood on tiptoe and locked both arms around his neck. "Will you skate with me, Flip? I'm really good."

Flip gave the sober members of the crew a let's-humor-them look, then reached into his own wallet for enough cash to rent the skates. He crammed Ronnie's money back inside her pocket before making her put on her jacket.

The wind whipped around the corner of the rental booth and Flip wished he'd brought a knitted cap to pull down over his ears.

Somehow they all got their skates on and wobbled out to the ice. Ronnie obviously had more skill than the rest of them, but the beer had done little to enhance her balance and Flip ended up holding on to her more for her support than his own. They made several laps around the rink, but never without falling and laughing hysterically every time they did.

Besides adding bruises to backsides, the outing seemed to clear everyone's head a bit. Except Ronnie's. Marsha had just taken another fall when she grabbed Flip's pant leg as he went past. His feet flew out from under him and his butt hit the ice soundly as he slid several paces beyond Marsha. Turning around, he crawled toward Marsha and finally struggled to his feet, then bent to help her up. Ronnie had ignored the whole episode and was attempting spins in the center of the rink.

"Good God," Marsha grumbled as Flip hoisted her to her feet and escorted her to the rail. "How could you guys let me do this? I have children. I could break my neck." Marsha held on to the rail and hobbled over to the nearest bench. "Barbara, help me get out of these damned things. I don't feel so good."

"Barbara," Flip said, "can you guys take Marsha back to the hotel?" Nodding to the center of the rink, he added, "I'll see that Nancy Kerrigan out there gets back safely."

The battered crew seemed more than eager to trade in the blades for their shoes and had hailed a cab before Ronnie became aware of their departure.

"Come on, Trenton Maxwell Farrell. Let's twirl." She waved to him from the rink center and actually did a fairly decent spin. "Trenton Maxwell, look at me."

She attempted a backward jump when her blade caught and she tumbled to the ice. Flip's heart almost stopped. Her intoxication had turned her into a daredevil, and while Flip wanted to shake her, he was more than intrigued.

He skated as fast as he dared toward Ronnie, but by the time he reached her, she'd managed to upright herself, seemingly without serious injury.

Flip held out his hand. "Come on, *Nancy*. I think you better sit this one out."

"How'd you ever get such a fancy name: Trenton Maxwell Farrell?" Barely keeping her balance, Ronnie slumped against Flip, wrapping one arm in his. "It sounds like a b-b-butler. Were you named after a butler, Flip?"

"Maxwell was my maternal grandfather's name, and he wasn't a butler. Mike's middle name is Terrance after my dad's dad. Being twins, we both got stuck with the grandfather's names. I'm T.M.F and he's M.T.F. His initials stood for *Much Too Fun* and mine were *Too Much Fun*." Flip grimaced, "Mother thought it was cute."

Looking at Flip, Ronnie affixed a mock serious expression on her face. "It is cute," she said, then dissolved into giggles again. "And really awful."

Ronnie let Flip escort her to the rail, where she leaned back and looked up at the Boston skyline. "Look—all the buildings are going 'round and 'round."

Flip didn't think he'd ever seen anyone so lovely, even if she was three sheets to the wind. Her hair was blowing free and her eyes actually glistened. He wasn't sure if it was the reflection off the ice or the fact that they weren't really focusing, but they were extraordinary.

Her cheeks were pink, just like they'd been when she'd come back from the hike with his mother. He liked the way she looked: healthy and beautiful. More importantly, he thought, she looked happy. She was like a child at play. It was incredible—the icy blonde wearing ice skates had begun to thaw in this freezing winter weather. He could only hope that some of the playfulness and happiness would remain when the alcohol haze had lifted.

After three tries, Flip managed to get Ronnie's card in the door lock before she fell over. While she'd seemed to recover some sobriety, now she was almost falling asleep standing up.

"Okay, let's get you on the bed; then I'll be out of here." Flip maneuvered her to the bed and gently let her slip out of his arms onto the mattress. She hit the bed and giggled as she bounced up a few inches.

Flip freed her from her jacket and tossed it on the chair along with her purse and scarf. He pulled off her leather boots and, feeling her icy cold feet, began a massage to warm them.

Looking up at her face, partially covered by silky strands, the urge to kiss her overcame him. It wasn't that he would go any further and it wasn't like they hadn't kissed. They had. Once.

Gently brushing the hair from her face, he bent forward and touched his lips to her forehead, her flushed cheek, finally her mouth. He hadn't intended more than a quick, soft touch.

Quickly, he became aware that his kiss was being reciprocated. And the way it was being returned was neither innocent nor tentative. Her lips parted and her tongue pushed through, darting and teasing in its exploration. He responded with more than his lips when she slid her hands under his jacket and pulled him closer to her. Her nails raked his back up and down in a rapid flourish of movement. His knees slid from a crouched position until he was lying prone next to the melting icy blonde. Wriggling out of his jacket, he pulled her closer, savoring her taste, her scent and her total meltdown.

~~~

Ronnie rolled over and pulled the covers up to her ears. There was a humming noise she couldn't block out. It echoed in the background of the bass drums that were beating back and forth inside her temples.

Slowly, she opened one eye. All that was visible was a bare foot. It upset her because she couldn't remember when she'd grown black hair on her big toe. Cautiously, she lifted her other eyelid. The brightness assaulted her and the drums beat louder and faster. She quickly slammed both eyes shut. Shielding them with a one-handed visor and squinting through slits, she struggled to sit upright. The sheet slid down and she was shocked to find she was naked from the waist up. She yanked the sheet up to her neck with her free hand and peeked underneath to discover she wore only her panties.

Carefully, she turned her attention in the direction of the bare foot sticking out of the covers. It wasn't hers. Her gaze traveled from the toes up the form under the blanket to the partially exposed broad back and masculine head of thick, ruffled hair. She didn't have to see his face to know she shared her bed with Trenton Maxwell Farrell.

"Oh God," she whispered. She prayed it wasn't "Too Much Fun."

In spite of the cymbals that joined the drum roll in her head, she inched her body toward the edge of the bed. Sliding one foot down to the floor, she took care not to disturb her sleeping companion.

Seeing her knitted shirt on the carpet, she grabbed it and quickly pulled it on. It didn't matter that it was inside out, she was just grateful the neck opening was large enough to fit over her watermelon head. She slid her other foot to the floor, then lowered her entire body. Head down, she crawled on her hands and knees along the edge of the bed, looking for the rest of her clothes. At the foot of the bed she ran into something solid. Lifting her head, she came face-to-face with Flip.

"Good Morning, Miss Kerrigan." Flip smiled. "Did you sleep well?"

Her champagne-colored satin bra with the lacy insets dangled from his index finger. "Looking for this?"

Trombones and trumpets joined the five-piece band clamoring inside her head as she looked into those amused gray eyes. The corners of his mouth tilted upward, and mentally she gave him five points for not laughing out loud.

"Hi, uh I uh seem to be…having some problems. I'll be back in a minute." Ronnie sprang to her feet and ran to the door of what she sincerely hoped was the bathroom.

Once there she turned on the water in the shower, stripped off the two articles of clothing and stood under the cleansing spray of warm water.

Hearing Flip yell something through the door, she cut off the water and yelled, "I'm fine. Please go to your room and I'll call you when I'm decent."

Oh God, what a poor choice of words. Decency evidently went out when her clothes came off.

Flip answered good-naturedly, "Okay. If you're sure you don't need me any longer, I'll go on down to my own room." Ronnie couldn't tell if it was the television or Flip, but through the closed door she heard laughter.

~~~

Ronnie spent more time than usual preflighting the airplane. She checked the controls, engine latches and tires. Then she walked to the other side of the plane and rechecked everything for a third time.

It was so cold she couldn't feel her feet, and if she stayed on the ramp any longer, she'd probably be facing amputation. She knew Flip and the rest of the crew had to be on board by this time.

She'd left word with the desk clerk to notify Flip that she'd taken an earlier shuttle bus to the airport. How was she ever going to face him? And the rest of the crew—what did they know?

Fortunately, Flip had been true to his word and had already left her room when she'd finally emerged from the bathroom that morning. She'd hidden from everyone else until it was time to fly out.

It wasn't as if she'd never had a hangover before, but she'd been young and silly then. At that age, one was expected to make stupid mistakes. But she'd never before had a night when she couldn't remember everything. Unfortunately, the things she did remember from last night did little to raise her opinion of herself.

Unable to delay any longer, Ronnie ascended the stairs to the flight deck. Entering the heated plane was a mixed blessing: It gave her the warmth she craved, but her hands and feet began to itch and tingle. She wondered if it was the heat making the sensations or her nerves.

Marsha, in dark sunglasses, rushed toward Ronnie as she was hanging up her coat in the crew compartment. She immediately thrust a steaming cup into Ronnie's hands.

"Here. This is herbal tea with lemon and double sugar. While it can't be the hair of the dog that bit us, it'll have to do." Ronnie accepted the tea gratefully, as much for the warmth of the cup as for the ingredients.

Ronnie felt Marsha's scrutiny but took one more gulp before she raised her eyes to meet the dark lenses of Marsha's shades. "Thanks, Marsha. Are you okay?"

Marsha pulled her sunglasses down and revealed two blood-shot eyes. "Outside of feeling like someone put my head in a vise and knowing I made a complete ass of myself in front of the entire crew, yeah, I'm fine. How about you?"

"I've got the band from 'Music Man' still practicing in my frontal lobe," Ronnie said, then drained her cup and smiled weakly. "But at least I can stand on my own now."

"I am so glad we have a direct flight home, and I am fervently praying this is Walt's night to take the kids to Indian Guides at the Y."

Ronnie couldn't bear the suspense any longer, and though she knew it was a big risk, she had to know if Marsha knew where Flip had spent the night.

"Uh, Marsha? Have you talked to Flip? I mean, did he say I was a total basket case or…you know, how does he feel about what happened?" The pounding of her heart replaced the faint sounds of the retreating band.

"What happened?" Marsha's eyebrows rose above her dark glasses. "He said you were funny," Marsha answered.

Taking Ronnie's empty cup, Marsha started for the galley, then turned around and added, "He did say the two of us shouldn't have gotten so blitzed and that he had a heck of a time getting you to bed."

Ronnie felt the color drain from her face. Oh my God, what did he tell Marsha? "What—what exactly did he mean by that?"

"I don't know." Marsha shrugged and continued, "He said you wanted to keep on skating, doing twirls and jumps and all kinds of stuff. He was afraid you were going to injure yourself."

Checking her watch, Marsha patted Ronnie's arm as she squeezed past her to return to the cabin. "I better help Barbara and Stan now. I owe them big time for getting me off the ice before I ended up in traction."

~~~

Flip was seated, headset in place, when Ronnie finally entered the flight deck. The flight deck computer had been activated and a printout weather sheet lay on her seat along with a travel packet of aspirin and Alka-Seltzer.

As she removed them and took her seat, she fumbled with her harness, finally locking the strap in place, and reached for her headset. Flip reached his hand across until it came to rest on hers and he held it until she met his gaze.

"Good morning again." He grinned, and while he knew he should have felt guilty knowing Ronnie was so embarrassed, he couldn't help but enjoy her dilemma. It was obvious to him she thought they'd done more than sleep in the same bed. God knows it had taken every bit of his will power not to act on impulse. Especially when she'd performed the impromptu striptease before passing out. Flip felt almost sorry for her when she finally found her voice.

"Good morning. I guess you got my message. I wanted to get here early…preflight everything…"

She glanced at the printed form. "I see you've already pulled up the weather."

Business as usual, Flip thought. "Nothing happened," he said before she crawled back into that deep freeze. "Ronnie, relax."

Ronnie's eyes widened and Flip watched her face cloud with bewilderment as she repeated, "Nothing happened?"

Her apparent relief reminded him just how much control she demanded of herself and how awful she must be feeling for losing it.

"I owe you an apology. I can't offer any excuses for my behavior except that I shouldn't drink." Ronnie's eyes darted away from Flip's intense gaze, but he could sense that tears were close.

"Hey, no big deal. I'll have to share some of my exploits sometime. But, Ronnie, next time you decide to drink, don't do it with beer and whiskey chasers until you've practiced up a bit."

He touched her cheek with his open palm and when she turned in his direction, his heart almost melted with emotion. She looked so vulnerable. Even hungover, she was the most beautiful woman he'd ever seen.

"How did I…did you… How did my clothes come off?"

"Ronnie, you undressed all by yourself." He stroked her face and was rewarded with a smile.

He decided she didn't need to know her act would have made Gypsy Rose Lee look like an amateur. "I hope you know that I would never take advantage of you like that."

She nodded and he could see that she was relaxing for the first time since she'd sat down.

"The only reason I stayed was because you were threatening to call room service. I didn't think I should leave you alone in your, ah, liberated condition." Flip watched with amusement as Ronnie hid her face behind her palms.

"Before I knew it, I'd fallen asleep, too." Pulling her hands from her face, Flip continued, "Ronnie, I slept in my jeans. If you don't believe me, I'll show you the marks the waistband made digging into my skin all night long."

"No, that's okay—I believe you." She didn't know if she should thank him or apologize. "Does anyone else know…anything?"

Flip chucked her chin playfully and handed her the checklist. "It's nobody's business but ours. Now let's get this bird in the air and go home. Ground control's telling me everyone has boarded."

Flip adjusted his headset and acknowledged the hand signals he'd just received from the Global employee standing in front of the jet. "We'll be getting push back in just a few minutes."

Flip smiled as Ronnie transformed herself into the professional pilot and began to read the checklist. Flip responded, and as the tractor pushed them away from the gate, Ronnie clicked on the PA system and delivered her cabin announcement to the crew and passengers.

~~~

They settled into a comfortable flight. Flip was respectful, courteous and funny. Ronnie appreciated the confidence he seemed to have in her as he relinquished more control in the flight deck than she'd ever imagined he would.

Why was he doing this? Could she be sure they hadn't had sex? *What am I thinking? Of course we didn't!* She knew she'd never been so drunk in her life and never would be again. Obviously, *she* was not one to be trusted.

Was he?

"Ronnie"—Flip's deep voice broke the silence that had settled over them for several minutes—"my folks are having their annual Thanksgiving bash. Since we both have the day off, I wondered if you'd like to come?"

Flip's invitation challenged her doubts, and while she didn't want to admit it, Ronnie was thrilled by the thought of spending another day in that beautiful setting with Flip's family.

It certainly would be different from the Thanksgivings she'd spent with her mother in some dreary cheap café or worse—alone while Mom entertained a new beau somewhere. Was that the reason for her elation? Or was it the thought of being with Flip that quickened her heartbeat?

"That's really nice of you to invite me. Mom and her husband decided to hit the casinos in Vegas so I didn't really have any plans. Are you sure it's okay with your parents?"

Flip leaned forward, adjusted a dial, then answered, "Of course. I wouldn't have asked if it weren't. My dad loves to show off his cooking skills. You'd be doing him a favor."

Ronnie scanned the rows of instruments above their heads. "I'd love to come. Ask your dad what I can bring."

Flip grinned and Ronnie appreciated his smile in a way she'd not allowed herself to at their first meeting. It didn't seem phony at all. It was warm and bright and wonderful.

Watch it, girl, she cautioned herself mentally. You have a goal to meet and a man isn't included in it—even a gorgeous man. Ronnie snatched another look at Flip's profile and could have sworn her heart flip-flopped inside her chest.

Don't be silly. I'm not a schoolgirl with a crush on the quarterback.

Then quit acting like one.

She promised herself that for the rest of the month, she'd be professional, courteous and, of course, she'd have to be friendly. She could be friendly without being mushy inside every time he looked at her or spoke or smiled. Sure, she could do that.

Couldn't she?

Chapter 7

The aroma of roasted turkey engulfed her as they stepped through the double front door. "We're here." Flip juggled the fruit salad Ronnie had brought and the two bottles of wine, which Ronnie had also selected. It turns out, despite his offer, that Flip's knowledge of wines was limited to color.

"Welcome. Happy Thanksgiving," Ken answered from the kitchen just as Ginny came into view from the staircase. Flip lifted his nose into the air and let it follow the scent of cooking food around the corner and into the kitchen. Ginny grinned at her son as he barely acknowledged her on his passage to the kitchen. Winking at Ronnie, she said, "Well, so much for 'Hi, Mom, you look well, kiss my foot or go to hell.'" She continued down the stairs with a petite female at her side.

"Mom, don't tell me you're still hoping the terrible twins are actually going to develop manners or class."

Ginny tugged an auburn curl of the young woman beside her, frowned in mock seriousness and said, "Hush, Gloria. Don't scare Ronnie away; I like her." Her grin widening, she put her arm around her daughter's waist and steered her toward Ronnie.

"This is our daughter, Gloria. She's gracing us with one of her too-infrequent visits. Gloria, please, let's have one day without twin trashing."

Ronnie unzipped her jacket. "I'm happy to meet you."

"Same here. I may have to retract my statement."

Ronnie felt uncomfortable as Gloria gave her a head-to-toe scrutiny. She was used to people ogling her, but not boyfriends' little sisters. *Boyfriend?* Where did that come from?

"Nice jacket. My brother may finally be showing some taste other than what's in his mouth." Gloria bounced down the last few steps and shook Ronnie's extended hand.

As she followed her daughter down the stairs, Ginny rolled her eyes, but not before Ronnie caught the twinkle.

"You'll have to forgive Gloria—she's a fashion coordinator for a large department store and I'm afraid she grades everybody on their apparel."

"Well, Mom, face it: The twin tyrants are fashion disasters. Lucky for them they wear uniforms on the job. It's just refreshing to see that Flip is seeing someone who has real style."

Shrugging out of her leather coat, Ronnie suspected Ginny enjoyed her daughter's good-natured digs at her siblings. "We're happy you were able to join us, Ronnie. Let me hang that up for you."

Ginny turned from the young women and hung the jacket on the antique coat rack against the wall.

Ronnie caught Gloria staring intently at her, brown eyes squinting. "You look familiar. Oh, my God. You're Miss Florida. What in the world are you doing here with my brother?"

"No, I'm not. I mean I was, but that was a long time ago. I don't think about it and I seldom talk about it."

It was obvious to Ronnie that Gloria did want to talk about it.

"You beat me in the 'Escape to Paradise Contest.' Remember—we both played the piano. I stumbled over 'Clair de Lune' and you killed them with Rimsky-Korsakov's 'Flight of the Bumblebee'."

Ronnie recognized Flip's sister now. She remembered how badly she'd felt when Gloria had played so poorly. The girl had been doing well, but stage fright had taken over in the final hours and she'd flubbed her talent portion.

"Mom"—Gloria intercepted her mother and pulled her back into the conversation— "Ronnie was in the 'Paradise Contest' with me. She won it by like a zillion points."

"My goodness, I believe you're right." Ginny smiled at Ronnie, and like her daughter, she squinted for deeper scrutiny. "I thought there was something familiar about you the first time I met you."

Ronnie tried her best to be gracious while they complimented her talent, her poise and everything else it took to win that stupid contest.

They couldn't know how much she'd wished someone else had won. With the trophy in Ronnie's hands, her mother had gone on a crusade. The idea that her little girl, just a month past her nineteenth birthday, would be a star continued—still continued, even now, as far as her mother was concerned.

"Don't get me wrong," Ronnie spoke quietly. "The pageants were fun, but they aren't a part of my past I'm particularly proud of."

She didn't want anyone in the kitchen to overhear this conversation, especially Flip. She'd had a hard enough time earning respect for her pilot skills without him knowing she was a beauty queen. It would just be one more item to add to the list of why she couldn't be taken seriously.

"The prize money was great and paid for a lot of flying lessons. But my mother was the power and the force pushing me on stage. I never enjoyed much of it."

"But you were the talent and the beauty. You did so well we kept track of you for a while." Gloria squeezed Ronnie's arm. "Why are you doing this boring, hard job with my dumb brother?"

Ronnie smiled at the idea anyone could think flying with Flip boring. Even if it was tedious at times, it had become even less so when she shared the flight deck with Gloria's "dumb brother."

"I guess that coming from a flying family, you might think it mundane, but truly it isn't. When I'm up there, well, I can't explain the thrill. But please don't say anything about the beauty contests and all that."

She waved her hand in a gesture of non-importance and stated, "It was just a means to an end for me and I don't want to do it again."

"Yeah, me neither." Gloria linked her arm in Ginny's and said, "But, Mom, I am sorry about all that money you spent on gowns and lessons and then I just quit."

"Well, it was a good experience for you. I never really minded as long as you had some fun with it."

Ronnie couldn't believe her ears. Her mother had been a fire out of control with every ribbon or trophy and title. And still was. Despite Ronnie's continued refusal, her mother sent off for every entry form available.

"You won't say anything to Flip, will you? I think he'd really tease me a lot."

"Well, you do know my brother, don't you?"

"Now, Gloria, you be nice." Ginny wagged her finger under her daughter's nose. "Try not to start a war with your brothers today. Please."

"Hey, are we going to get any help from the women in this tribe?" Ken hollered from the kitchen doorway. "Isn't it enough that we have to hunt and kill the game? Do we have to cook it by ourselves, too?"

"Ken Farrell, when's the last time you hunted down anything?" Ginny yelled back, then grinned at the girls. "I guess we better go lend a hand. It sounds to me like they're popping the beers already."

~~~

Flip opened his eyes. "Ooh, I'm too full," he moaned, then rolled off the sofa and struggled to his feet.

From his relaxed position in the burgundy leather recliner, Ken Farrell looked affectionately at his son. "What'd you expect? Two pieces of pumpkin pie with double whipped cream and a *sliver* of pecan pie?"

"Don't rub it in." Flip groaned, stretched and looked around the room. "Where's Ronnie?"

Mike came in with an armful of wood, which he unloaded carefully in the box near the hearth. Tossing two medium-sized logs on the fire, he glanced over his shoulder and answered his twin.

"She's with Mom and Gloria—they're doing a nature hike or something. She took off after getting a look at you sprawled out and snoring." Mike grinned. "A flea-bitten coyote would look more noble than you did on the sofa."

Flip walked to the window and peered out. "It looks cold out there."

"It is." Mike jabbed at the fire with the poker and flinched as the sparks flew up the vast chimney. "I checked the weather reports and there's some activity brewing in this area."

Frowning as he watched the tall pines sway in the side yard, Flip's face sobered. "Do you think I ought to go look for them?"

Ken raised an eyebrow in Mike's direction. "I think your mother will see that they don't wander too far off the beaten track."

"What's the deal, man?" Mike placed the poker back in the stand and closed the screen. Directing his full attention on Flip, he remarked, "This is the second time in less than a month that you've brought Ronnie up here. So is this a serious thing? Is my brother actually thinking of commit¬ting to more than just an R.O.N. relationship?"

Turning from the window, Flip glared at Mike and growled, "I've never had a Remain-Over-Night relationship—well, almost never anyway. Besides, you're one to talk."

"Hey, I'm not throwing stones, just curious."

"Both of you stop it." Ken got up from his chair and threw the magazine he'd been half-heartedly reading on the floor. Flip remembered that serious look and tone of voice from his childhood, but it'd been a long time since his father had used it.

Ken's gaze drilled one son and then the other. "I know the industry doesn't exactly encourage committed relation¬ships, but I'm here to tell you, it's too damn bad it doesn't." He strode toward the kitchen, then turned and continued in a quieter voice, "Both of you are single and, from what I've heard, have no problems attracting women. Believe me, I understand how tempting it is, but eventually you get tired of coming home to empty rooms." Ken paused and unexpectedly chuckled.

"What's so funny?" Flip hadn't expected his father to exhibit any humor right in the middle of what seemed to have been a serious lecture.

Ken met Flip's gaze. "I don't really know if I need to tell you this, but when either of you start contemplating marriage, you need to know there's lots of turbulence in this industry that can crash a marriage."

"Believe me, I seen the wreckage. That's why I'm never anxious to make the leap," Mike quipped.

"But, you see, Mike, you may avoid some storms but you miss out on the thrill of soaring, too." Ken returned to his chair and, resting his arms on his knees, folded his hands in front of him.

"Sometimes even the smallest slip can ground a marriage. I remember back when I upgraded to captain, and I hate to admit it, I was pretty full of myself." Still grinning, Ken said, "Well, I guess I was pretty obnoxious because your mother sewed four stripes on my pajamas and my underwear and packed them in my bag when I left on a trip."

"And that almost ruined the marriage?" Flip couldn't believe his father would have let a little humorous joke have that much power.

"Oh, no, that was just your mother trying to put things into perspective. It's funny now, but at the time, I felt she didn't appreciate my status. She was more interested in whether I could make the Little League games or Gloria's ballet recital."

Ken's hands tightened into fists as he continued, "On that trip, I was tempted more than I'd ever been in my whole life. I won't go into details, but suffice it to say that it was an expensive trip. What you build on your own turf is worth so much more than a few stolen hours of forbidden excitement. Keep your professional life separate from your personal life."

Mike cleared his throat as if to speak, but fell silent instead. Flip looked at his dad and realized that this was as much information as they were ever going to have on the subject.

Ken clapped his hands together and stood up. "So when you boys find the right one, for God's sake, don't mess up. I think Pickles needs a walk." Whistling for the dog, he quickly exited the room.

"Wow, what was that all about?" Mike left the hearthside and plopped on the sofa.

"I think that was a warning or a confession." Flip settled down into the chair his father had vacated, then leaned forward, elbows resting on his knees, fingers laced together.

"Mike, do you remember that summer we spent with just Mom on Cape Cod?"

"How could I forget? I filled Nana's bathtub with sand crabs and beach critters. They all died, and jeez, it stunk to high heaven."

Flip chuckled at the memory. Gloria had felt sorry for the creatures and gave them a bubble bath. Collecting his thoughts, he continued, "I think Mom and Dad were having some problems then.

I wondered why Dad was never there. Remember how Mom cried a lot? I bet she'd left him."

"They must have put it together somehow, but it was strained for a while. Of course, we were what? Ten? Eleven? We weren't exactly tuned into adults and their activities, but I do remember missing Dad. When you think about it, they are the exception. How many pilots do you know who're still on their first marriage?"

"Why do you think I've always run the other way?"

"Yeah, me too. But Mike, don't you get tired sometimes of always having to be on guard?"

"What do you mean?" Mike looked puzzled and yet Flip knew he'd peaked his brother's interest.

"Well, for instance, you meet someone and you're definitely attracted." Flip pushed his hair off his brow and struggled to find the right words. "First you're afraid to approach them, and then when you do, you've got to make sure you don't come on too strong until you know if you even want a relationship."

"God, bro. You make it sound like work." Mike slouched back against the sofa. "Listen, with me, the girls know that nothing is forever. We have fun, a few laughs, but when it gets to the talk of houses and cradles, I am out of there in a New York minute."

"So that doesn't get old? Are you saying you're not tired of it?" Flip leaned back in the chair.

Mike shrugged. "I try not to think about it and just live in the moment."

"I don't know. I see these kids who belong to this one FA. Those little guys are a kick." Flip grinned as he thought of Marsha's two little boys and made a mental note to visit them soon. "I think sometimes it might be fun to have somebody to come home to. Jeez, Mike, we can't have a dog or even a goldfish. There's no one in my house but me. And I'm gone half the time."

"I think she's got you, man." Mike threw a sofa pillow in Flip's direction.

"Who?" Gloria burst into the room. "Who's got Flip?" she demanded, then bounded behind Flip's chair and slipped her hands around his neck.

"Holy Mother Fu—" Flip spun from his chair and caught his sister by the waistband of her jeans.

Her giggles turned into screams. "Mom! Come quick—Flip's killing me."

"It'd serve you right." He knuckled Gloria's head, but released her promptly upon seeing Ronnie standing behind his mother.

"Jeez, Gloria, you just about gave me frostbite. Your hands are like ice." In spite of his statement, a warm flush crept from his collar to his forehead. Embarrassed, he rubbed his neck and grinned at Ronnie.

Hands on hips, Ginny shook her head. "Ronnie, can you believe my children? All of them in their thirties and they act like juveniles."

"I'm not thirty yet," Gloria protested.

"Yeah, well, more stunts like that and you'll be lucky to make it to thirty," Mike quipped from his station on the sofa. "It should be obvious that not all of the Farrell offspring are as mature as the eldest twin."

"Hey, all of you, enough with the insults." Ken Farrell appeared out of nowhere. "Mike, if you have to be in San Juan tomorrow, you might want to check on your connection. It may be iffy since it's a holiday weekend."

"Dad, I'm holding a ticket. If the commercial flight is cancelled or delayed, it's not my fault."

"Still, you might want to check and see what's going on before you leave."

"Okay"—Mike propelled himself from the sofa—"but either way, it's no big deal." Finishing his sentence, he went to the den to make the phone call.

"We probably should go, too." It was obvious to Flip that his father had had about enough of sarcastic humor for one day.

"Daddy, we're sorry. We'll behave." Gloria wrapped her arms around Ken and was rewarded with a return hug. "I was hoping we could hear Ronnie play before they leave.

~~~

The drive home had been relaxing. Flip glanced over several times at Ronnie snoozing as the late afternoon sunshine faded into purple and orange hues the closer they got to the San Diego coastline.

He made the last turn onto Crown Point Boulevard before Ronnie sat up and blinked. "Oh my gosh, we're almost home. Have I been asleep all this time?"

Flip grinned as he watched her check out her makeup in the visor mirror, combing her fingers through her hair. "I'm afraid so, and you snore, too."

"I do not." Ronnie turned abruptly and Flip could not help but chuckle at her indignation. She actually bristled at the idea she could snore.

"Okay, maybe not snore exactly, but you do mumble a lot." Flip watched her eyes widen and he wondered if anyone had ever watched her sleep before. Obviously she'd never shared a room with a sibling like he had.

When they'd shared a room, Mike had never failed to report Flip's sleep activities to the other family members. Every time Flip snored, belched or farted, he could count on Mike to blab and embellish. He'd even told Dad about the most embarrassing event of Flip's preteen years: the first wet dream.

Ronnie realized he was teasing and finally relaxed enough to tease him back a little. "Even if I did snore, which I don't, I could never hold a candle to you." She enjoyed seeing his discomfort. His jaw dropped and she knew she'd hit a target.

"Yes," she went on, "I understand that sometimes you have chased the birds out of the trees. Mike said you scared them once into thinking an earthquake was rumbling around somewhere."

"Well, I might have known Mike had something to do with your opinion."

Giggling, she touched his arm and was surprised when he took her hand in his and held it on his thigh. She had wanted to touch his strong legs ever since she'd seen them in those form-hugging Levis. She had to admit, the warmth she felt through the soft worn denim was more than pleasing to the touch. He applied the brake and she felt his muscle tense, sending her pulse racing, her heart pounding. Intense heat spread all over the rest of her body.

She was having more trouble than she'd ever dreamed trying to be cool and professional around this man. Every smile, every touch, every look was putting her at risk of losing her composure.

"Here you are, safe at home."

Ronnie reluctantly pulled her hand from his lean limb and tried to speak. Nothing came out. She swallowed and tried again. "Would you like to come in," she rasped, cleared her throat and finished, "for a drink or—" She realized she had nothing to offer but mineral water and herbal tea.

"Sure, but we better take in this food that Mom pawned off on us." Flip reached back behind his seat and grabbed the two plastic bags filled with makeshift cartons of leftover Thanksgiving dinner. "God, I hope none of this stuff leaked. Mom won't give me her Tupperware after I forgot to return it and tossed it out."

It was too late to back out, and while Ronnie was apprehensive about extending her time with Flip, she couldn't deny her excitement.

It would be fine, she told herself. She'd be able to handle this gorgeous, sexy hunk in her house for a short while…alone. She wasn't one to fall all over any man. Even gorgeous, sexy, kind and funny hunks.

~~~

Flip leaned against the counter in the immaculate kitchen, drinking the bottle of the mineral water Ronnie had given him. He could have gone for a beer, but it was either the water or the herbal tea and, frankly, water had more kick than that anemic tea. The thought of not staying simply didn't occur to him. She was finally warming up some and he needed to see if she was capable of reaching any point beyond tepid.

Her kitchen was spotless—like a laboratory. Everything was either stainless steel or white porcelain. Two kitchen towels hung from the oven handle, one white and one burgundy and green plaid. In the small alcove that served as an office, there was a miniature vase with tiny silk flowers, also in shades of burgundy, pink and green.

He thought about the dirty dishes he'd left piled in his sink, the half-empty can of beer in the bathroom and the mail he'd dumped in the middle of his unmade bed.

"It was the best Thanksgiving I ever had," Ronnie said as she transferred the leftovers Ginny had sent into small plastic containers.

Carefully she labeled each square or round vessel. "Your mother sent enough food for a month. I'll just put them in the refrigerator until you're ready to go."

"I can't take that stuff home."

"Why not? It's wonderful that she shares with you."

"I tell you what, you keep the food and I'll come over here to eat it with you." Flip slipped his arms around her, holding her in place. Her hands fluttered over the containers as he tightened his embrace.

This had been just about the best day he'd ever had. He pulled her close against his chest and noticed that her eyes were closed. He watched the goose bumps prickle her arms as he nibbled her ear and neck and finally spun her around to face him. He kissed her softly and then deepened the kiss. Still she didn't respond. He teased with his tongue and finally she began returning his kiss.

~~~

Trying her best not to let her emotions take over, Ronnie fought the urge to react and encourage his advances. It was a losing battle. Thoughts of the uneasy intimacy he'd managed to instill in her on the ride home assaulted her brain. Helpless to block out the fantasy of lying with him in bed and letting her hands wander over the rest of his hard body, she felt her breath quicken and her pulse was off on a marathon again.

The thought of sleeping with him at last was overwhelming. She wanted that experience. She was sick of denying herself. Well, she'd actually slept with him before, but that didn't count because she'd been completely passed out. It still humiliated her to think about Boston. Was all this touchy, feely stuff coming from him because she'd let him take liberties she couldn't remember?

It was as if someone had taken her out of the safe zone and she was helpless to do anything but plunge forward into…she didn't know what.

Letting her guard slip even further, she laced her fingers in his hair and drew his mouth to hers. All reservations, self-consciousness and inhibitions seemed to melt away and suddenly she had the insane urge to free him of his clothes.

He obviously had the same idea as her sweater was tugged over her head and flung somewhere she couldn't see. He buried his face in her cleavage; his teeth nipped playfully through her satin bra as her nipples stood at attention.

Her heart surged and she truly hoped that all her healthy habits had made it strong because she felt as if it could burst with pure joy. She let him explore her upper body and became more impatient, pressing her torso closer to his.

"Ronnie, I need you." His voice broke with huskiness.

Speaking in a whisper, she told him where her room was, then gave a short hop and wrapped her legs around his waist. Taking one hand from his neck, she quickly undid her bra and let it slip to the floor as he carried her down the hall.

Pushing the door fully open with her foot, she blew gently in his ear and nibbled his neck before they fell across the queen-sized bed.

Ronnie watched Flip yank at his shirt buttons while she struggled to get her jeans off over her boots. The damn narrow legs now trapped just over the heel of the boots wouldn't budge. She could only imagine how she must look, struggling like a four-year-old when she so wanted to look sexy, desirable and smooth. She should have kicked them off before she got this far.

Flip pulled his shirt, half unbuttoned, over his head, then reached down and removed Ronnie's boots and socks. In a quick swoop, his hands grasped her thong panties and pulled them free of her body along with the jeans.

Towering over her, he gently touched her face, fondled her breasts, then slowly unbuckled and slid out of his jeans before lowering himself to her side.

Her body screamed for relief as she melted into his arms and pressed against him. Desire clamored throughout her as he gently stroked her hair, kissed each eyelid and licked the pink nipples that now throbbed in unison with her hot center.

She clawed his back as she tried to force him to move faster, cover more territory and satisfy her need to be filled.

"Now, please now." She moaned, squirming and reaching between his thighs in her effort to persuade him to give her satisfaction.

"Soon," he whispered and pulled away from her long enough to get protection. For what seemed like hours, he was gone from her side and doubt skittered into her thoughts. Did he leave her like this for a joke? Had she pushed too much? Returning, he manipulated the condom package while she gratefully accepted his kisses and soothing, reassuring voice.

Starting at her chin, he kissed his way down her belly to the juncture of her thighs. She could almost hear the sizzle of her body as his tongue touched her skin.

Just when she thought she couldn't bear it any longer, he entered. The entire Metropolitan Opera with full orchestra and extra violins gave a special performance in Ronnie's mind in honor of her glorious climax.

Chapter 8

Ronnie had never felt so deliciously satisfied or happy in her entire life. Stretching across the bed, she ran her hand over the pillow where Flip had rested his head, then let her fingers walk down lazily to the sheets where his body had laid claim to hers.

The whole evening had been so incredible that if it weren't for the shirt strewn across the chair under the window and the faded Levi's lying on the floor, she would have thought she'd dreamed it.

She'd heard girls from the pageants and even in the crew room at work talk about "getting it" more than once, but until last night, she'd thought it was just bragging and giving more credence to sex than it deserved.

Now? Now, she wanted to tell everyone that she was a multiple-orgasm chick. And it was all due to one hot hunk who belonged to her. Her thoughts were so basic, they embarrassed her, and frankly, the idea that Flip belonged to anyone was absurd.

Oh God, what if she was just another one of his conquests? She'd talked his ear off last night until she'd had to admit exhaustion. She'd even told him she was going to call his parents and get a list of his favorite recipes and learn to cook all of them. What was she thinking? She couldn't get all gooey and domestic now. Could she?

~~~

Flip lathered under the spray of hot water and winced only slightly as it landed on the scrapes left by Ronnie's fingernails. She'd been a tiger in bed, and though he'd always thought of himself as somewhat of a he-man, she'd damn near done him in. Even after all the incredible sex, she'd still been full of energy. She'd suddenly started telling him some long and convoluted story about one of her classmates in flight training, and then kept apologizing for talking too much. It was hilarious. He hoped she'd do it again. There was still so much he didn't know about this girl.

He sniffed the pink bar of soap. God, he was going to smell like he'd been to the spa for a beauty treatment. It was probably wonderful for a woman with skin soft as velvet, but perfumed flowers and honeysuckle scent definitely didn't fit the he-man category.

He'd laughed when Ronnie had given him a pink plastic razor, a new toothbrush and a few other necessities imprinted with various hotel logos. His mother had obviously made an impression on her that first visit and she'd come home and duplicated the convenient little packages.

He stepped out of the shower and onto the fluffy white bathmat. There were two snowy white towels on brass rods, folded in triplicate and hung precisely the same distance from the floor. The brass fixtures glowed as an example of what polishing and care could render. The overhead fan drew the steam up and out of the bathroom and Flip looked at his reflection in the unfogged mirror.

What was I thinking? Was I thinking? She likes my family and I obviously gave her the impression I want a serious relationship. This is not a girl who takes things lightly.

Flip continued to carry on a mental conversation with his mirror image, but the more thoughts he had about leading Ronnie astray, the more the idea of settling down seemed logical. After all, he was thirty-five and he'd been ten when his dad was that age.

What am I waiting for? Love? What the hell is that anyway?

The flimsy little toss-away razor gave his beard a once over and the final results looked like he'd lost a fight with a pair of hedge clippers. He'd nicked himself in three different places and the cleft in his chin had been a challenge. Finally, he wrapped one of the fluffy towels around his waist and poked his head out of the bathroom.

"Hi. I wondered if I was going to have to come in and rescue you." Ronnie's gaze took in Flip's body from the top of his still-wet head to his long tapered feet. She lingered a bit on the area around his belly where a small patch of hair began its downward path, disappearing beneath the towel. Forcing her eyes to meet his, she smiled and said, "I'm glad to see you didn't drown."

"If I had been in that kind of danger, would you have given me mouth-to-mouth?" he teased.

"Actually, I've heard just thumping a person on the chest is as good a way to start the heart. That mouth-to-mouth stuff might be on its way out."

"That would be a shame." He crossed the short distance separating them and by the time he reached the bed, the towel was one more item cluttering the normally neat bedroom.

~~~

"I don't know about you, but if I don't eat something, I'm going to expire from hunger." Flip peeked at her from his half-closed lids. She was cuddled under his arm and he'd been right: That long blonde hair looked great spread out on a pillowcase.

"Hmmm," Ronnie stirred and looked up, snuggling even closer. "Me too, but I don't have any food in the house."

"What are you talking about?" Flip sat up, dumping her unceremoniously on the pillow. "My mother sent enough for six crews and fourteen dead-headers. You jump in the shower and I'll zap lunch in the microwave."

Scrambling around, Flip found his jeans and shirt and padded barefooted out to the kitchen—something he didn't do at his place unless his cleaning lady had made an appearance. His kitchen floor tile was a color that camouflaged dirt, which was both good and bad. Good in that he didn't have to worry about it looking clean, and bad because he was always stepping in something gooey that had blended in so well with the tile.

Finding everything he needed to make up two blue-plate specials of turkey, dressing and candied yams had not been a problem. Ronnie had marked each container and dated it. It seemed unnecessary to him that she took the time to date it. Usually he just tossed stuff into the fridge and if it hadn't turned blue or smelled rank, it was edible. Most of the time, it turned blue.

The microwave buzzer dinged and he started to remove the first plate when he noticed the minutes still clicking on the built-in timer. The buzzer sounded again and he realized it wasn't the oven but the front door.

"Ronnie, someone's at the door. Want me to get it?" Not hearing an answer, Flip wiped his hands on one of the pristine tea towels and went to answer the door.

The woman digging into her purse had yet to look up. "This must be the wrong key, but it's the one I had before—" She raised her head and stared at Flip. Though her jaw didn't exactly drop open, it drooped at each corner about the same amount of distance her eyes widened.

"May I help you?" Flip wasn't sure if the matron with the overdone makeup was lost, selling something or in need of assistance. Her platinum hair was showing a good half-inch of brunette roots and the texture was something akin to straw.

"Who the hell are you?" she snarled. Eyes as blue as Ronnie's scrutinized him. "What's happened to Veronica? Oh my God, did she get married?" Something resembling a smile of sorts flittered across the woman's face only to be replaced almost immediately with a frown. "Why didn't someone let me know?"

"No, I—uh, wait a minute. I'll go get Ronnie." He didn't know whether to ask her in or shut the door and unfortunately his hesitation gave her just the time she needed to push him aside and gain entry, dragging a battered suitcase that whacked Flip in the knee as she passed him.

"Veronica. Are you here?" She spun around and confronted Flip. "So, do you have a name?"

"Yes, I'm sorry, I'm Flip…well, actually it's Trent Farrell. I'm a friend of Ron—uh, Veronica's." He extended his hand and the unexpected caller put her suitcase in it.

"Flip? Are you watching television? It sounds like someone's in the house." Ronnie came into the living room wrapped in her terrycloth robe, her hair twisted up in a towel. Flip watched her face lose the rosy glow from her shower and turn the same shade as the white towel around her head.

"Marlena! What are you doing here?" Ronnie clutched the lapels of her robe and wrapped the other arm tightly around her waist.

"What? No 'Hello, nice to see you'?" Squinting at Ronnie, the visitor continued in a tone edged with sarcasm. "I understand now why you haven't answered my calls and why none of the pageants have any record of your entry. You've been busy." The woman switched her gaze from Ronnie to Flip and then back to Ronnie. Flip felt as if he'd been caught with his hand in the cookie jar and was about to have it rapped with a ruler.

Nodding her head in Flip's direction but keeping Ronnie frozen in place with her eye-to-eye gaze, the woman said, "Well, do I get introduced or is he the butler?"

In a voice barely audible, Ronnie introduced the woman as her mother. Once more, Flip extended his hand and found it still held the suitcase. Hastily, he set the suitcase against the wall and gestured toward the sofa. "Mrs. Talbot, if you'll have a seat—"

Trying to rescue Ronnie the only way he knew how, with politeness and charm, Flip guided the visitor to the living room.

"It's Mrs. Jenkins. For the time being anyway." She looked Flip up and down. "I can see my daughter has good taste in men. You are a hunk." Her smile broadened. She winked and said, "And you can call me Marlena." Plopping on the sofa, Marlena opened her purse and pulled out a small mirror.

"It's a pleasure to meet you, Marlena," Flip said as he struggled to know what he should do next. While Marlena checked her makeup, Flip made eye contact with Ronnie and with exaggerated facial expressions, motioned her to do something.

Ronnie looked like a scared little rabbit cornered by a hound. She stood glued to the floor until Flip moved to her side and slipped his arm around her waist. "Ronnie, why don't you sit down too? Maybe I could bring you some tea?"

"No, Flip, stay. Please?"

Flip's uneasiness was nothing compared to the look of intense pain on Ronnie's face. Could this hard, harsh person really be Ronnie's mother?

Ronnie had scarcely mentioned her mother the few times she'd even ventured into the subject of her family. He'd had the impression doting parents with lots of loot had raised her. This woman was not anywhere close to doting and as for having a comfortable lifestyle, the battered suitcase and dark roots disputed that idea.

Flip directed Ronnie toward the loveseat across from the sofa and sat down with her as Marlena snapped her compact shut and drilled them with a cold, hard stare.

"So, Veronica, is this young man special or have you succumbed to a casual living arrangement?"

"Flip isn't living here. We fly together and I spent Thanksgiving with his family."

Marlena gave Flip another intense inspection, one that left him feeling scorched by her eyes.

At the risk of being labeled a coward, Flip decided to bail out of the situation. "Ronnie, I think I'll run along now. I'm sure you and your mother have a lot of catching up to do."

"No, Flip, stay. You haven't eaten," Ronnie protested.

"Hey, no problem; I'll grab something. I'll call you later." He excused himself and hoped her mother wouldn't find it strange that he retreated to the bedroom to collect his shoes and the rest of his belongings. Before he made his escape, he hastily smoothed out the comforter and plunked several decorator pillows of various shapes on top of the bed. The spread hung a foot lower on one side, but it looked more presentable than it had just minutes before.

~~~

Ronnie couldn't blame Flip. She'd have liked to bail too. She wished she had a trip to go on. Maybe she could act like she did. Would her mother know the difference?

"Marlena, what are you doing here? I wasn't expecting you. You said you were going to Vegas for the holidays."

"Veronica, you wouldn't believe what I've been through. Phillip is a toad. An unfeeling, selfish, lying toad." Marlena pulled a used Kleenex out of her oversized purse and blotted her mascara-laden eyes with the only corner without a lipstick imprint.

Ronnie suppressed a sigh. Same story, different man. For as long as she could remember, her mother had been trying to find Mr. Right. There had been the series of bankers and professional men when Ronnie was young, but as she got older, the caliber of her mother's boyfriends and husbands deteriorated. Mr. Jenkins supposedly was an investor. Ronnie learned only too soon that what he invested in mostly was the ponies, a roulette table or other games of chance. Obviously it'd been a while since he'd had a winning streak. Ronnie noticed her mother no longer wore the diamond ring she'd flashed around when she'd become Mrs. Phillip Jenkins just under two years ago.

"Of course I couldn't stay with him. I guess you'll have to put me up for a few days until I get on my feet. That's not going to be a problem, is it Veronica?"

Ronnie looked at the woman sitting next to her and remembered when she'd believed every word that came out of her mother's mouth. It was hard not to. Her mother had been so beautiful and so persuasive. Success and fame were always just around the corner, just a week away; the proverbial ship was always just about to dock. But it never did.

Ronnie had been shuffled from one school to another, and when she was old enough, she'd been paraded across stage after stage, winning titles her mother had assured her were going to launch them into stardom.

"Of course you can stay." Ronnie patted Marlena's knee. She couldn't throw her out on the street—although the men Marlena had been with never had a problem doing just that.

"Veronica, are you and that young man living together?"

Ronnie couldn't understand why it would even cross Marlena's mind to inquire such a thing. God knows her mother had always had men living with her for as long as Ronnie could remember.

As soon as she'd learned to talk, she'd been instructed to call her mother by her first name. By the time she was ten or eleven, she'd figured it out. Marlena passed her off as a little sister instead of her child. Marlena used to say, "Age will kill a career as quick as a bad script."

That early on, Ronnie had decided she would never put herself in a position of having to rely on any man for anything.

Maybe that's why she'd worked so hard to break into flying. It was still a man's world, but she wanted to be one of the women who forced it to change. And she didn't want to lie about anything to attain her status either.

"No, Marlena, I don't believe in that. You know I've always enjoyed having my own space."

"Well, that's true. You've always been a loner." Ronnie felt Marlena's gaze intensify and was steeling herself against the expected onslaught of criticism.

Instead, Marlena surprised her with an outburst of good-natured chuckles. "Well, good for you. I did something right, didn't I? I raised you to be a proper lady."

Ronnie smiled and thought of all the people she'd patterned herself after instead of her mother. The chaperone at the first junior pageant had taught her how to dress and use her makeup in a subtle way instead of layering it on, as her mother was prone to do. She remembered the piano teacher who had guided her talent as well as taught her how to carry and conduct herself on stage. Poise and grace were not birthrights—they had to be learned.

"Marlena, you did a lot right. I'm just sorry things haven't gone well for you."

Somehow, in those early days, her mother had always found money for the lessons, the dresses and the traveling expenses. Ronnie didn't even want to think about what her mother had done to accomplish all that.

"Oh, honey, I may be down, but I'm far from out. I just talked to my agent a few weeks ago and he's looking for a part for me now." Marlena fluffed her hair and smoothed her skirt. "Actually, Phillip was holding me back. I tried to settle down, but you know, honey, show business is in our blood."

Ronnie caught that familiar look in Marlena's eye and her heart ached. Her mother would always live in her own special dream world.

Standing, Marlena swept her arms upward. "We have to be in the lights or we'll fade into oblivion." Pulling Ronnie from the loveseat, Marlena said, "You still have time, Veronica. You are beautiful and talented and I know one day your name will be in lights."

"Marlena, please." Ronnie pulled away and bit her lower lip to keep it from trembling. She turned her back to her mother and stared out the window. She'd had this conversation numerous times on the phone, but she'd never had the courage to face her one on one.

It was the only thing Marlena had ever wanted: stardom. When she'd failed to achieve it, she was determined her daughter would make it.

"Marlena"—Ronnie grasped her mother's hands—"I know what you've always dreamed for me, but it can't happen. I don't want it to happen."

"Veronica, don't be silly. It's what you've worked for all your life." Marlena shook off Ronnie's hold and paced between the sofa and loveseat. "This silly flying thing, well, I let you blow the bucks on training, but only because I thought you'd get it out of your system."

She stopped in front of Ronnie, grabbed her by her shoulders and shook her vigorously. "Veronica, it's time you go back to your destiny: show business, movies, modeling, something besides a ton of metal that will probably crash and kill you."

"I'm sorry. I can't be what you want me to be. I never really was." Ronnie slumped to the sofa and pulled her knees up under her. The towel on her head unwound and fell to her shoulders, revealing a slightly damp, tangled mass of blonde hair.

"My God, when was the last time you had your hair trimmed? It needs shaping badly." Marlena stepped closer and fingered the tips of Ronnie's hair.

"To hell with my hair. Mother, haven't you listened to a thing I've been trying to tell you? I am not going to be an actress. a model, a beauty queen or a hooker like you—I'm a pilot and a damn good one."

The minute the words were out, she wanted to swallow them back. The look on her mother's face told her she'd finally gotten her attention, but was it worth the price?

"Marlena—Mom, I'm sorry. I didn't mean that. I just—"

"Veronica, may I put my things in the bedroom?" Marlena squared her shoulders, strode to where her bag sat against the wall and gestured with it as she said, "It's that way, isn't it?"

When she reached the hallway, she turned and met Ronnie's gaze square on. "I'll try to get my affairs in order as soon as possible and then I'll be on my way."

Without another word, Ronnie watched her mother leave the room with all the dignity of a star performer at the end of the closing act.

Chapter 9

Grateful that she was scheduled for a four-day trip, Ronnie stocked the refrigerator with food her mother found more acceptable than Mrs. Farrell's holiday leftovers.

Ronnie had to admit, for a woman whose face took makeup magic to hide the passage of time, Marlena's figure had the firmness of a much younger woman. Every morning without fail, Marlena did a series of exercises and bullied Ronnie into joining her.

Ronnie lifted her packed carry-on, suppressing a groan as her sore muscles objected. "Mother, I'll call you when we get to our first destination and give you the hotel number."

Ronnie was so anxious to leave the condo, she almost felt guilty. For three days, it had just been the two of them. The guilt Ronnie felt over her misspoken words had been milked for all it was worth at every opportunity. Marlena acted as if every day she remained at the condo was pure torture, but Ronnie noticed she had no problem helping herself to cosmetics, clothing or anything else that caught her eye.

Marlena, wearing one of Ronnie's robes, sat on the sofa filing her fingernails. She'd not had much to say since breakfast and seemed to ignore the whole idea that Ronnie was going to work.

Focusing all her attention on her nails, Marlena spoke in a nonchalant tone, "I'll be fine. If this deal works out, I'll be on my way to New York, or there's a chance something in Hollywood will gel."

Finally, she turned to Ronnie and, in a voice as cold as her stare, said, "I gave my agent this number. I trust that's permitted?"

Trying hard not to wish her mother gone when she returned, Ronnie managed a smile. "Of course it's okay, and, Mother, I left some cash on the dresser if you need anything…I mean, until your finances get settled with Phillip."

"That's not necessary." Her mother went back to concentrating on the bottles of Red Alarm and Screaming Pink nail polish, and Ronnie cringed as she watched Marlena juggle them around on the arm of the white sofa.

"Well, I better go. I'll call." Ronnie waited but there was no response. Folding her London Fogger over her arm, she wheeled her luggage out the door.

They were doing the Boston trip, then short hops on the East Coast out of Boston to Philly and then an overnight in Toronto. The last day was a long one with stops in Ohio, Phoenix and, if they kept on schedule, on into San Diego. If weather or mechanicals became a part of the picture, it meant delays.

Ronnie expected to be the first to check in and was surprised to see Flip waiting for her in operations with a cup of café latte— something he'd convinced her was just as good for her as herbal tea and tasted a whole lot better.

What was he doing here? He hadn't bothered to call, and while that could be due to the shock of meeting Mom, he still could have sent a text or something to let her know he was thinking about her. But maybe he wasn't. Had she imagined the intimacy she'd felt growing between them?

Her heart picked up the tempo as she met his gaze. Gray eyes capable of drilling holes through people looked at her now with such compassion and concern they weakened her knees. Handing her the cup, his fingers lingered and stroked hers until she was sure she'd spill the contents. He didn't kiss her, but she could tell it was a struggle for him not to. As for her, she wanted to throw her arms around him, bury her head into that special curve of his neck and shoulder, and let him carry her off to some secret, secluded, safe place.

Instead, they took care of business, got the weather reports, did the walk-a-round inspection of the aircraft and boarded before the rest of the crew arrived.

The trip was long and bumpy. Thunderstorms across the Ohio valley had kept the flight attendants busy with passengers turning various shades of green every time the aircraft hit turbulence.

Checking into the hotel, Ronnie signed the register. All the rooms assigned to Global were on the same floor.

Janet, the redheaded siren, had been the lead attendant on the flight. She'd spent more time popping into the flight deck than she had taking care of passengers. Flip had been polite, but unlike Ronnie, he seemed unaware Janet was on the prowl.

It was more than obvious to Ronnie. Especially when Janet had been brazen enough to suggest to Flip that they could save the company money if she gave up her room and stayed in his. Flip had laughed, playing it off as a silly joke.

Ronnie hadn't seen any humor in it at all. Janet was so blatant that it was embarrassing to everyone. Besides making her uncomfortable, it made Ronnie want to claw Janet's eyes out.

But, of course, she'd acted cool and disinterested. She noted that the room assigned to her was directly across from Janet's and two doors away from Flip's. What would really put that man-chaser in her place would be if Flip took Ronnie and her luggage directly to his room.

Of course that was out of the question. Flip was probably sorry he was stuck with her for the rest of the month. After all, he hadn't even called since he'd left her condo three days ago. It was obvious any interest he might have had was squashed by her mother's appearance on the scene. He probably would end up with Janet tonight.

She'd seen the shocked look on his face when she'd introduced Marlena as her mother. He couldn't relate and she couldn't blame him. His idea of a mother was Ginny Farrell—sophisticated, educated, gracious.

Stuck in the air for hours, it'd been impossible to ignore the subject of her mother's visit. As painlessly as she could manage, she'd given him the short version of her life. Unknown father, mother bent on stardom, lots of schools, lots of stepdads and/or "uncles" and very little structure. Now he knew more than she'd ever wanted him to know.

He hadn't said two words in the van on the way to the hotel. She could only imagine how he'd react if he had all the gory details of her life.

~~~

Flip punched the remote and the channel changed again. He'd gone through every station, yet nothing held his attention. God, he was confused. He'd never in his life turned down free, hot sex with a looker like Janet before. Was he sick? Could he be lovesick? He'd never had a woman get under his skin, into his head and grab onto his heart like Ronnie.

The story of Ronnie's life still rattled him. She'd delivered it in monotone, as if she were giving clearances for landings. It was so sad and pitiful, and yet something told him not to show sympathy—she'd definitely take it the wrong way.

Instead, he'd been quiet. Maybe that was enough. He wasn't sure what she felt for him. He knew she was crazy about his family and now he knew why. She never even had a childhood.

He'd tried to imagine her as a little girl. How lonely she must have felt. No wonder she'd crawled inside the covers of books and escaped into music. She'd created a life that didn't resemble her true existence.

He wanted her to stay with him that night, but she'd seemed so fragile and ragged that he didn't want to presume he knew what was best for her. If she'd given him one bit of encouragement, he might have made the suggestion. But all he'd seen was a sad, quiet shadow of the Ronnie he'd spent the night with less than a week ago.

He'd called every day, but she'd never returned his calls. Marlena always told him Ronnie was out or he got a busy signal, which meant she'd forgot to put it back on the stand again. The attempts calling her cell weren't any better. He wasn't sure why.

The television blurted out the local news report, cutting away for commercials at measured intervals, but Flip couldn't have repeated what was flashed across the screen. He just stared at the images and thought about the first day he'd seen Ronnie.

"Boy, my first impression was way off the charts," he mumbled aloud. "No doting rich daddy and silver spoon for that lady."

Piecing together the little bits Ronnie had revealed about her childhood and his observation of her mother, he was starting to understand why Ronnie had seemed so distant and cold.

She'd been used and abused, maybe not physically, but there are worse hurts than a smack in the chops. He thought of his own childhood—he couldn't remember ever having felt the kind of pain and fear he'd seen in Ronnie's eyes.

His mother's flyswatter had stung his backside lots of times, but it had almost been a joke. He'd yelp loud enough that his mom usually stopped before she'd really made any lasting impression. Their father had disciplined him and Mike both, but usually the fuss was over by the time he'd gotten home, and punishment ended up being manual labor.

Dad's favorite chore was painting the fence around the pool. It was made of rough pine slats with cross-timbers and the job took forever. Usually, they'd make a start and then their dad would relent. The consequence, like the famous Northern California bridge, was a fence that was never one shade of paint. It never got a complete coat of paint at one time. It became a family joke and was called the Golden Gate fence as long as they lived in that house.

His parents had always meant love and safety. Just looking at Ronnie told him she'd never felt safe, and he wondered if she'd ever felt truly loved.

Clicking off the set, Flip picked up the phone and punched in Ronnie's room number. He wasn't sure she was ready to see him, but he couldn't wait any longer. He wanted to let her know…what? He was there for her. Was he? Before he could analyze his last thought, a soft voice came over the receiver.

"Hello?"

Besides being barely audible, Ronnie's voice held a sadness that pulled at his heart. He was determined to bring back the spark that had begun to melt his icy blonde when she'd given herself to him.

"Hi, gorgeous. Please tell me you haven't had dinner."

"Flip?" The surprise in her voice intensified the emotion gripping him. Did she think he wouldn't call her after she'd told her life's story? Did he come off so shallow?

"Yep, it is I, starving and in need of pleasant company. Do you want to go out or join me here and I'll get room service." His gaze drifted across the large bed. Just imagining her lying next to him sent his lower body into a spasm of sensation and expectations.

"I—I didn't expect you to call. You seemed tired."

Flip pulled a pillow under his head and adjusted the phone. "Yeah, I was, but now I'm refreshed and I think you and I need to talk."

Had he caught her just out of the shower dressed to go out, or was she still in her uniform, too tired to change?

"I've really said everything necessary and I understand how you feel. I'm fine, really."

The cool, icy tone was back, and while it made Flip sad, it also made him angry as hell. He'd be damned if he'd let her crawl back behind that wall of cold indifference. He'd seen Ronnie heated up with the fun of living and he didn't want that doused with ice cubes before it even got fully ignited.

"Well, I'm not fine. How come you didn't return any of my calls?" He grabbed another pillow and jammed it under his head with the first one.

"This is the first call that's come to the room."

"I don't mean here, at the hotel. I've called you every day since your mother arrived. Didn't she tell you? I didn't even have luck with your cell. Does it need a new battery or what?"

There was a pause; then Flip heard what could have been a sob or a sigh. "Ronnie? Are you okay?"

The response was garbled, but Flip got the important part. He heard her say, "I'll be there in five minutes."

It was the longest five minutes of his life, but when he opened the door she was standing there in her London Fogger. She'd pulled her hair back with a clip and scrubbed her face clean of makeup. She was a vision of perfection. At least to him.

"Aren't you going to let me in?"

He realized that while he'd stood there taking in all that he deemed lovely, he'd blocked her entrance. He moved to one side and she shuffled in wearing a pair of light blue terrycloth slippers. This was not the sophisticated first officer who never let her guard down, knew FAA regulations forward and backward, and landed jets in turbulence without mussing a hair. Flip had never seen Ronnie look so beautiful or so vulnerable.

Ronnie padded over to the club chair near the desk and plopped down. She slipped out of her coat and arranged it on the back of the chair. She crossed her arms over her chest and sat primly with her knees touching.

Flip's gaze locked on Ronnie's satin pajamas. The top could pass for a blouse. It was modest with covered buttons and a delicate rose embroidered on the pocket. The bottoms were short, exposing her legs from high thigh all the way down. Just looking at them made Flip want to slide his hands up and down the smooth texture covering her firm hips and buttocks. He wondered if she was wearing anything underneath. He hoped not.

"So, I'm guessing by your attire you'd like to order in?" Flip shut the door and sat facing her on the edge of the bed.

Her gaze met his and once again the crystal clear blueness of her eyes sent him soaring. And yet he always felt their deepness hid so much.

"If you want to go out, it's okay."

"No, we'll eat here. I'd rather not battle a crowd."

Did she tuck her toothbrush in her coat pocket? Oh, what the hell, she could use his. He just knew he couldn't let her leave tonight. Somehow he had to let her know he understood—*he* would be there for her.

~~~

Ronnie had been grateful that Flip didn't push for any more information. He busied himself with room service and ordered more than ample food for two. He made silly jokes and she'd found herself smiling. He was gentle and kind.

He tilted her chin and looked into her eyes. "I like you without makeup."

"I look awful." She started to cover her face when he stopped her and kissed the beauty mark on her upper lip.

"I can't understand why you only have one of these when you are so incredibly beautiful."

She blushed at his compliment. But he'd succeeded in getting her to relax. She was beginning to trust him. Maybe he was different than the other men she'd known.

She owed Flip an explanation. "I didn't get any of your calls. My mother must have intercepted and I found my cell phone dead under my bed. I had no idea how it got there until now.

"Flip, I want you to know I'm not ashamed of my mother."

Even as she spoke the words, she knew it was a lie. That was exactly the reason she'd come unglued. Her mother was an embarrassment. Because of her mother, she'd worked so hard to become perfect.

Driven to excel in school beyond the point of normal studies, she did everything she could to learn as much as possible before she'd have to change schools. Fate had given her a quick mind and she used it. Marlena had only wanted her to use her looks.

"I never thought you were." Flip chuckled. "But you've got to admit, you may be the one person who can contradict that old adage about the apple not falling fall from the tree."

Flip picked up their dinner tray and put it outside the door. Closing the door, he turned around and said, "Honey, you and your mom aren't even planted in the same orchard."

"Well, Marlena's had it hard. I know she'd never planned on being a single mom." Ronnie moved onto the bed and sat cross-legged, her back against the headboard.

"She never told me much about my father, but I think he was pretty smart. I've always had a passion for math and figures. Marlena's never balanced her checkbook. When it gets really bad, she changes banks."

"Well, that sounds pretty smart to me. At least it did when I resorted to that method once."

"You too?" Ronnie couldn't help but giggle. "Is that true or are you just trying to make me feel better about Marlena."

"It's good to hear you laugh." Flip eased down on the bed beside Ronnie. His arm brushed her bare leg and, in spite of all the self-talk she'd done about not letting herself get involved with him again, a shiver danced up her spine.

"My life has been so different from yours. I know you can't understand how it is with Marlena." As if she needed a barrier between them, Ronnie grabbed one of the bed pillows and held it across her chest. "Your family is so—so normal. I mean, you have parents who love each other after forty years. Even with all the fussing and scrapping, I know you, Mike and Gloria would go to battle for each other. I don't know anything about that."

She didn't want to look at him because she was afraid of what she might see. The last thing she wanted was a relationship built on pity. She'd been on the right track at the beginning. No encouragement, no relationship. No relationship, no confusion or distractions.

"I don't know whether to smack you or kiss you." Flip grabbed the pillow out of her grasp and held her by the shoulders. "But since I've never hit a woman and never intend to, I guess I'll have to kiss you."

He pulled her to him and planted a deep kiss on her lips. Her head tilted backward by the force of his kiss. One hand left her shoulder to cradle her nape while the other arm encircled her body and they slid into a melded prone position on the bed.

He didn't push or demand but rather, let her set the pace—returning kiss for kiss and only taking what was offered. Ronnie fought to keep a rein on her passion, but having him close, inhaling his scent, made her want more. His muscles responded when she stroked her fingers over his arms and shoulders. Her breath, now short gasps, barely kept pace with the pounding of her heart against his chest.

She meant to call out his name, but the sound was more like a moan, then a sob, as she reached for his shirttail and yanked it over his head. He paused for just a moment and then slowly he removed her pajama top and the matching shorts. Kissing away the tears that slid down her cheeks, he maneuvered his jeans over his hips and kicked them the rest of the way to the floor.

Ronnie clawed his back, nibbled his ears and silently cursed him for taking so long. He continued to stroke and kiss her. His tongue blazed a trail from her lips to her nipples. He sucked and nibbled until Ronnie thought she'd explode. Just before she did, he entered. Deep and slow, then faster until his passion and strength were also spent.

For what seemed like a long time, they lay just as they had finished. Neither moved until it was evident that his weight was becoming uncomfortable for her. She squirmed to ease the heaviness and he hoisted his body up on his elbows, freeing her upper body but not releasing his claim.

Looking up at him, she smiled. "I definitely vote for your kisses. But what did I say that made you think I needed a smack?"

"Because you acted like I'm a snob." He didn't raise his voice. His tone was firm and he continued to stare her down. "You're actually the snob. You think you can concoct an image and a wall so thick, no one will break through. Then no one can hurt you."

Ronnie saw his stare soften into compassion. But not pity. He cupped her chin and gently kissed her. "Ronnie, I can't promise I won't hurt you. In the real world people are hurt all the time. But I'm starting to think that if we don't allow ourselves to risk because we don't want to get hurt, we end up missing out on the joys of life and love."

Her eyes brimmed and she fought to keep her mouth from trembling. For the first time, she wondered if she'd finally met a man who spoke the truth.

"Flip"—her voice shook but she forced herself to speak her piece—"we met not quite two months ago and yet I've thrown myself at you more times than I care to remember. I'm not like Marlena, but I've done nothing to make you think otherwise." Not wanting him to confirm her statement, she shut her eyes and turned her face into the pillow.

Flip sighed and rolled onto his side of the mattress. He made no attempt to leave the bed or cover himself. "Boy, for a smart girl, you sure say some dumb things."

Ronnie turned to face him and struggled to keep her eyes on his face—although it was a challenge. That beautiful male body had blended so perfectly with hers that she'd almost been sorry when they'd climaxed.

"Ronnie, there is nothing *that* wrong with your mother. She's not exactly the bridge club and ladies' tea social variety, but look at you. Ronnie, you have more determination than almost anyone I know. That had to come from somewhere. Maybe your mom?" He reached out and traced a finger down the side of her face, stopping just below her ear to caress a silky blonde lock of hair. "Only someone who really cared would have worked so hard to see that you got a chance to discover your talent."

"She didn't do it all for me. She found out I could do something that was marketable. She needed me to live her dreams, not mine." Ronnie grabbed the sheet and pulled it up over her. Even if he was comfortable in the nude, she wasn't. "Now that I've sold my piano she's really mad because I'm too rusty to enter those stupid contests."

She took a deep breath and looked at Flip squarely, which took more concentration than she'd imagined. "With flying I can support myself. Performing is fickle. I don't want to depend on agents who think they own you, producers who want to use you and audiences that expect too much."

"But, still, you gotta give Marlena some credit. If nothing else, she made you dig down deep inside and find something you loved more than the piano."

"But, Flip, she's still trying to make me do it her way. She never told me you called. Because you're a pilot, she would rather you disappeared. She wants me to give up my career."

The tears began to spill down Ronnie's face and Flip saw her fight to stop their journey. He took a corner of the sheet and blotted them away.

She grinned at him and he responded in kind. "I'm silly, I know. It'll be okay. Marlena's not a witch." Then she giggled, "Well, not all the time anyway."

"Maybe there's some way we can convince her that flying is really a good choice." Flip stroked Ronnie's arm and laced his fingers with hers. "What can I do to make her think I'm a hero?"

"There's nothing really. Unless you can get her a job in show biz, Marlena may be my permanent roommate."

Ronnie sighed, and then tossing a pillow, she arched her brows and said, "However, it might help to put some clothes on. Unless you want me to attack you shamelessly again."

"At last, my prayers are answered." Flip lunged for her, ripping the sheet away from her body. Before he devoured her lips, he reached over and extinguished the bedside lamp. Snuggling down in the covers, he joined Ronnie and added chuckles to her throaty giggles.

Chapter 10

The rest of the month seemed to zoom past and soon Ronnie's assignment with Flip came to an end. Ronnie was depressed and Marlena was still her roommate. The elusive agent had not returned her calls and it was becoming apparent that her mother might not be leaving for some time.

Flip had a new first officer and Ronnie had flown with a variety of captains. None of them were as competent, or as gorgeous, as Flip. She and Flip had managed to get together a couple of times for dinner and actually went to a movie, but their schedules varied and they were seldom off on the same days.

The holidays were approaching and the airlines were getting busier with kids coming home from college for the winter break, families traveling to visit relatives and the usual groups of business travelers trying to make that big deal before the new year arrived. The weather was still pleasant in Southern California and nasty back East, with more snowfall than the previous year.

Ronnie had gritted her teeth and was determined to enjoy the holidays in spite of Marlena's constant complaining about the no-good agent and the deadbeat soon-to-be-ex hubby. Ronnie had advanced Marlena the funds for filing divorce papers.

It seems she did actually marry Mr. Jenkins. But the divorce was more of a formality than anything else. There would be no property settlement. He didn't have anything. It was important that Marlena didn't get stuck with paying his debts, and the sooner the marriage was dissolved, the better.

Ronnie quickly hung the last of the ornaments on the small artificial tree. She was looking forward to Christmas this year as much as a six-year-old. While it had never been a huge holiday for her as a child, this year was different.

"So when are we going for dinner with your fella's folks? Christmas Eve or Christmas Day?" Marlena asked, sprawled in the middle of the floor doing leg lifts. Pulling to an upright position, she cocked her head and looked at the tree.

"What? What are you looking at?"

"You got a bare spot over there." One perfectly manicured hand pointed to the left. "Looks like you could use some tinsel or something."

Ronnie rearranged a few ornaments, then stepped back to view her creation. It looked fine to her. She didn't really know why she was bothering. She and Flip had already decorated a tree at his house, and she knew the Farrells would have a wonderful blue spruce or maybe a huge Douglas fir at their mountain home.

Marlena was the only thing that dampened Ronnie's spirits. In spite of her promises to be on her way to New York or Hollywood, she was still very much a fixture at Ronnie's condo. Ronnie couldn't see Marlena even in the same room with the Farrells. But how could she have Christmas there without including her mother?

"Marlena, don't get your hopes up too high. I may have to fly Christmas Day." Ronnie let the lie roll off her tongue as if she were used to it. What was happening to her? She was becoming someone she didn't even like, much less respect.

"Don't be silly. Who goes anywhere on Christmas Day?"

"I don't have time to explain the airline industry to you, but believe me, nothing is certain. You might want to make other plans, just in case."

"Well, it isn't like I know a lot of people here." Marlena stretched out her legs and flexed her ankles, then said, "Thank goodness, I've met a few of your neighbors."

"Who? Whom have you met?" It was a large complex and Ronnie wasn't one for lounging around the pool. She only knew the name of her nearest neighbors because the mailman had once delivered their mail to Ronnie's condo by mistake.

"Well, there's Mark O'Neal, Hal Corbett and another sweet elderly man, but I've forgotten his name. They've all been helpful driving me around. You never seem to be in town. But don't worry, Veronica—I'm sure it'll work out."

Marlena stood, stretched and ran her fingers through her scalp, fluffing the new bleach job. "I even got my hair done. Do you like it?"

Ronnie had to admit, it looked a lot better and not nearly as brassy as the day she'd arrived. "It's lovely. Did you do it yourself?"

"Oh no, I found your hairdresser's card by the phone and she worked me in. Rita said you could pay her when you come in for your trim on Friday. She's very good."

Ronnie couldn't believe her ears. "Marlena, why didn't you ask me first?"

She'd kept her appointments to a minimum. Friday was to have been her day to pamper herself and now she'd be lucky to afford a shampoo.

"Well, Veronica, I didn't think you'd mind. After all, I'm family. I've sacrificed for you for years. I thought you'd be glad that I want to look my best." Her expression changed into a whipped puppy face before she turned and quickly made her escape toward the bedroom.

"Family?" Ronnie muttered. "Oh yeah, Mom, we make a great family."

How many Christmases had she spent in cheap hotel rooms waiting for her mother? The holiday dinner sometimes consisted of cellophane packaged crackers and overripe fruit saved from the last meal at the local greasy-spoon café. Sometimes Marlena returned with bus tickets or cash and they'd head out for the next Miss Whatever contest. She never had a decent coat but the pink satin gown was always packed with care along with the matching pumps and the rhinestone jewelry. How she ever won anything had been a mystery to Ronnie until she was old enough to understand where her mother went while she waited.

Family? For the first time in her life, she was beginning to understand what it would be like to be a part of a real family. The Farrells were a family. They were normal people and they took care of each other.

Last week she and Gloria had gone shopping together. It felt like having a sister. Gloria had protested when she'd bought expensive gifts for Ken and Ginny. A leather-bound cookbook set for Ken and miniature Waterford crystal grand piano for Ginny. Ronnie ignored Gloria even though she knew her credit card was on the verge of being maxed out.

Marlena had upset her budget as much as her peace of mind, well before the buying of a few Christmas gifts.

Marlena had unpacked her suitcase and deposited her meager wardrobe in a small section of the closet, though she rarely bothered to wear anything that wasn't Ronnie's. The dry cleaning bill increased, as did the utility bills.

Ronnie casually mentioned she had an account at the health food store and almost went into shock when the monthly statement arrived. Marlena had charged several hundred dollars worth of herbs, youth-preserving vitamins, lotions, creams and minerals.

Ronnie knew she had to get out before she blew her top. Marlena was ruining everything for her. Battling anger and guilt whenever she thought of Marlena going to the Farrells for Christmas, Ronnie hoped against hope that something happened before Christmas Eve.

She even entertained thoughts that perhaps her mother would meet a new man between now and then. One who would take her to New York, Hollywood or anywhere, so long as it was miles from the Farrells' home.

The numerous irritations and the drain on her budget had a lot of influence on Ronnie's shopping choices. She'd bought Marlena a matched set of luggage for Christmas in hopes her mother would take the none-too-subtle hint.

Ronnie made no attempt to correct Marlena's assumption she was out of town most of the time. The truth of the matter was, she'd become almost as much a fixture at Flip's place as Marlena had become at hers. The difference was he seemed to be enjoying her presence.

Grabbing her jacket and purse from the hall closet, Ronnie yelled in the direction of the bedroom, "I'm going out."

She checked to make sure she hadn't left any business cards or credit cards lying around. God knows what else Marlena would decide to order.

Ronnie drove aimlessly when she realized she was on the highway to the Farrells' home. The mountains had gotten several snowfalls and enough was left on the ground to give the whole area a magical atmosphere.

Not wanting to arrive unannounced, Ronnie used her cell phone to call ahead. Assured that her visit was not an interruption, Ronnie disconnected and picked up as much speed as she could while still staying safe.

Parked cars lined the road, and beyond barbed wire fences, people played in the snow. Snowballs flew through the air while lopsided snowmen dotted the landscape. Kids on flattened cardboard boxes and plastic garbage can lids slid down small hills and tumbled into ditches.

By the time Ronnie turned into the Farrell driveway, her depressed mood had lifted and she grinned broadly as Ginny waved to her from the deck.

"You're just in time. I've been baking cookies all morning and I need help."

"Ginny, I've never baked a cookie in my life." Ronnie entered the house and knelt down to pet the cocker spaniel, which had bounded down the stairs yapping the minute Ronnie crossed the threshold.

"Pickles, quit pestering Ronnie." Ginny locked her arm through Ronnie's and guided her into the kitchen. "There's nothing to it. Come on—I'll get you an apron. We have to hurry before Ken gets back or he'll try to take over. I swear, the man thinks he's Wolfgang Puck."

Ronnie giggled, shrugged out of her jacket and tossed it on one of the barstools.

"I'm surprised Flip didn't come with you, but I'm also delighted. It'll give us a chance to girl talk." Ginny tied a "Kiss the Cook" apron around Ronnie and pointed to the sink. "You might want to wash up. Pickles had a run-in with a skunk three nights ago. We've tomato juiced him several times, but he still has that aroma."

"I wondered if that was a new doggie perfume. If it was, I was going to suggest you toss it."

She ran warm water over her hands and squirted liquid soap as she rubbed them into a lather. "Flip didn't know I was coming and, besides, he felt he had to go see Jack."

"Isn't that boy back to work yet?"

"Oh, yeah, his ankle's all healed and he's off disability but now his nose is out of joint."

"Excuse me?" Ginny said, as she went to work with her spatula on a pan of cookies.

"Well, Flip said that Jack expected to be scheduled with him as soon as he came back to work. But everything got rearranged with the holiday schedules. Jack won't be back flying with Flip until the New Year."

Ronnie accepted the cookie Ginny offered and between bites said, "I don't know how it happened the month I was scheduled with Flip, but was it a great schedule and sure beat being on reserve. Now, of course, everyone's flying with the increased holiday flights."

Ginny handed Ronnie the spatula and indicated another sheet of fresh baked cookies. "Slide those onto that platter and then I'll show you how to roll some out and cut them."

Wiping her hands on a dishtowel, she said, "Is that the only reason you liked the schedule? It beat reserve?"

Ronnie felt the color rising to her cheeks and she knew it was the question more than the heat of the oven. "Well, of course, I liked flying with Flip. He's good at his job and he's professional. I've learned so much." She slid the spatula under a snowman and broke his head into several pieces.

"Ooh, I ruined this one."

"No, it's not ruined—it's a sample now. I always need lots of samples. Otherwise Ken and the boys would eat all the perfect ones before Christmas." Ginny smiled and held out a plate with several broken cookies on it.

"Did I hear my name being spoken in vain?" Ken popped into the kitchen and kissed the back of Ginny's neck.

"Ken, you're freezing. Go away."

"No, warm me up." Ken grabbed Ginny around the waist and Ronnie lunged forward to rescue the platter as she watched the couple engage in a deep kiss.

Ronnie felt like a voyeur, and even though her face instantly warmed with the flush of embarrassment, she couldn't take her eyes off them. She'd felt passion with Flip, but this was different. This was like putting on a pair of comfortable slippers or snuggling up with a warm quilt and a favorite book. This was comfort, security and, for lack of better words, real true love.

Two more batches of cookies and several cups of tea later, Ronnie drove back to San Diego.

And back to Flip?

Could she and Flip achieve what Ginny and Ken had? She was glad Ken had interrupted when he had. Ginny was getting into questions that Ronnie had no idea how to answer.

Before she'd met Flip, men had not even entered into her plans. Not the immediate one anyway. Her goal was to fly the skies as captain in command. Was there room for anything else? Lately she'd been thinking a lot about that. But she still didn't have the answer.

~~~

"So, Veronica, what do you think?" Marlena twirled around in front of the mirror, then back to face Ronnie. Her platinum hair shimmered and the gold-toned braids on her bright red jumpsuit glistened as the mirror caught her reflection.

Ronnie's gaze slid down to the gold backless pumps on Marlena's feet and recognized them right off. She'd worn them once: to a New Year's Eve party last year. It had been one of the few social occasions she'd attended since she'd hired on at the airline. Her date had been a gate agent, and before the night had ended, she'd almost had to defend herself with the spike heels of the gold shoes.

Large gold hoops dangled from Marlena's ears; the matching bracelet on her wrist clanked as it ricocheted off the jacket's dime-sized brads. Ronnie also recognized the jewelry and caught the scent of her own perfume as Marlena made a second rotation.

"Marlena, this is a dinner at someone's home, not opening night at some club in Vegas."

"Are you saying you don't approve?" Marlena admired her reflection in the mirror, ran her hands down her trim waist and, with a pout Ronnie couldn't miss, she whined, "I got this number on sale at that cute little boutique around the corner. You shop there, right?"

"How did you pay for it?"

"They let me take it out on approval." She turned and faced Ronnie. "I was going to take it back if you didn't like it, but you're never home and now I've had it altered."

"You what?"

"That sweet little man whose name I can never remember has a wife who sews like a dream. She had to nip in the waist and skinny up the legs—I'm still a petite six."

"So how are you going to pay for it?"

"Well"—Marlena's mouth drooped into its familiar pout—"I thought maybe it could be my Christmas present."

Ronnie stifled a groan. "Fine, Marlena, keep the outfit. While you're at it, keep the shoes and the jewelry too." Ronnie was too tired to argue. It was bad enough that Marlena was going to look like one of the tree ornaments next to Ginny. The contrast would be so overwhelming, Ronnie was sure she'd never be included in any Farrell gathering again.

~~~

There were no emergencies that required Ronnie to report for a flight and Marlena didn't come down with the flu. Ronnie had loaded several bottles of wine, the special-ordered rolls from the German bakery and two containers of honey butter into the trunk of her car when Flip pulled up in his two-seater sports car. With Marlena added to the party, Ronnie's sedan was the logical choice for the drive to the mountains.

"Ooh, I wish we could take your sports car, Flip," Marlena crooned. "I bet it really hugs the curves." Ronnie's eyes rolled heavenward.

"Here, let me give you a hand with those." Flip moved to assist Ronnie.

Marlena wandered back to the sedan and leaned against it. "It's not going to be too cold up there, is it, Flip? Am I dressed warmly enough?"

Ronnie slammed the trunk with a bang, then tossed the keys to Flip. "You drive."

Flip caught the keys in mid-air. "I think you'll be fine. There's snow in the mountains, but if the sun comes out, it'll warm up."

"Marlena, get in the car. You aren't going sledding." Still seething, Ronnie watched her mother pout for a few seconds, then move toward the passenger door.

"Back seat, please," Ronnie barked, then looked up to catch Flip stifle a chuckle. Marlena hesitated for just a moment, then quickly climbed in the back seat of the sedan.

Ronnie took the passenger's seat next to Flip. She slammed her door and fastened her seatbelt with such a vengeance, she had to loosen it immediately or hold her breath for the entire drive.

Marlena chattered with Flip all the way to the mountains. Ronnie didn't think either of them noticed how quiet she was. *They* were having a wonderful time.

It was almost enough to make Ronnie want to feign a headache and turn back. Except she'd miss the Christmas tree, which Ginny said they'd grown right on their property. She wanted to smell the cedar and pine logs burning in the fireplace and eat Ginny and Ken's delicious food. This was the first Christmas when she'd been a part of a real family. More importantly, it was a day with Flip's family.

Pickles scampered across the deck, yapping as if guarding Fort Knox. Flip maneuvered Ronnie's car between other vehicles parked alongside the drive.

"My gosh, do you have this many relatives?" Ronnie's gaze took in the luxury cars, noting the Jaguar in particular. "I know Ginny said there would be family and a few friends but, Flip, this is a crowd."

"Knowing my mother, she probably got carried away again. She gets caught up in the spirit and ends up inviting people she met the day before."

"Well, this looks like my kind of party." Marlena popped her seatbelt and gathered her faux fur jacket around her. "Park this buggy, Flip. I can't wait to meet your family."

Flip barely had time to release his seatbelt and exit the car when Mike, followed by Pickles, bounded off the deck. The two brothers embraced in their usual manner of bear hugs, sharp jabs and faked belly punches.

Ronnie watched her mother's expression light up like an electric bulb, her attention riveted to the small group now gathered on the deck. Ginny's wave motioning for them to hurry caught Ronnie's eye.

Ronnie suddenly felt drab in her winter-white tailored slacks and matching turtleneck cable-knit sweater.

Ginny sparkled like tinsel on a tree. Her jade green hostess gown dipped in back at the hemline and plunged in front at the neckline. Accenting her cleavage was a gorgeous diamond pendant, and at her wrist she wore a tennis bracelet that reflected the afternoon sun every time she waved her hand. Between Marlena and Ginny, Ronnie looked about as dazzling as cold mashed potatoes.

~~~

"Veronica, do you know who that is over there by the fireplace?" Marlena was almost squealing like a teenager with excitement.

Ronnie glanced at the group of men poking the fire clutching either bottles of beer or mugs of eggnog. One in particular did stand out. He wore a diamond in his ear almost as bright as Ginny's pendant. His pants were so tight Ronnie was still trying to figure out how he'd managed to sit down for the wonderful dinner they'd just enjoyed without splitting a seam.

"Oh, Flip introduced me. I think he's in show business or something. They've been friends forever."

"Veronica, what planet do you live on? That's Cory Davis. *The* Cory Davis."

"And he is—"

"My God, how long has it been since you read a *People* magazine or turned on a radio station featuring something besides hits from the '80s?" Marlena huffed in disgust and leaned closer to her daughter. "Cory Davis is the hottest teen idol singer of the decade and oh, my God, he's coming over here."

Ronnie couldn't hide her surprise as the blond Adonis approached the women. He walked with the swagger of a confident bon vivant. He smiled at them and Ronnie thought Marlena might actually giggle.

Fortunately, she managed to contain herself as she extended her hand. "Mr. Davis," she bubbled profusely, "what a pleasure to finally meet you."

"Just Cory, please." He shook Marlena's hand, then turned to Ronnie, took her hand and lowered his lips to her fingertips. Ronnie could have sworn she heard Marlena sigh while she felt her face flush.

Pulling her hand free, she stammered, "So, you're a friend of Flip and Mike's?" Duh.

"Okay, back off Cory." Flip joined the trio. "Ronnie's not one of your groupies."

"Sorry, old man. I didn't know I was trespassing on your territory."

Ronnie couldn't wait to hear Flip's reply. What did he feel for her? Had Cory unearthed a spark of jealousy?

"It's not that exactly," Flip said and met Ronnie's gaze. "Ronnie's my copilot and one of the best. I don't want her taking a leave of absence to fly around the country with a two-bit singer and a teenage band."

"Excuse me, flyboy, but this two-bit singer went platinum on his last album with that teenage band."

"Flip, you really ought to respect Cory," Marlena chided. "My goodness, my agent says he's destined to become a legend. Just like Elvis." Marlena wiggled in between the men and locked her arm with Cory's.

"You have an agent, Marlena? What is it you do?"

"I'd love to tell you, Cory. Let's go sit down. You know, I could probably be an asset to your group."

Flip and Ronnie watched Marlena lead Cory to a secluded window seat at one end of the great room.

"So, I'm one of the best?" Ronnie turned and stared out the floor-to-ceiling windows at the winter wonderland Mother Nature had provided. A few months ago, Flip's compliment would have made her day—her year. Now she just felt like crying.

She felt Flip's breath on the back of her neck. "I don't want Cory to get the idea we're an item. It would only make you a target—he still thinks he has to compete with me."

He placed a hand on her hip and she fought to keep her excitement from escalating. Flip continued, "Cory has a warped sense of values. He doesn't understand that a career can mean more than just money. Besides, he wouldn't understand how a beautiful woman could be focused on flying."

Did Flip believe that was all she cared about? She'd once thought it would be enough. Now she wasn't so sure.

Chapter 11

Christmas decorations still adorned doorways and the flight crew mail slots, but the mood in operations was business as usual. The keyboards clicked and phones rang while schedulers cajoled and argued with flight personnel.

Although her flight wasn't scheduled to take off for two hours, Ronnie had arrived early to revise her manual. The holidays were over and Marlena had finally moved out.

Ronnie didn't know how she'd managed it, but somehow Marlena had convinced Cory Davis that she was just what his group needed to keep things running smoothly on his upcoming tour. She'd left with the group the day after Christmas with the dubious title of personal assistant.

Basically the job was that of a gopher, but to Marlena, it was her big chance. When she explained it to Ronnie and Flip, she'd made it sound like she was on the brink of stardom. Marlena could make keeping the hotel room ice buckets filled sound like an executive position.

Ronnie was happy for her mother and even happier to have her condo back. She did notice Marlena had no trouble filling up her new set of luggage. Some of the clothes Ronnie recognized and the rest she figured Mai's Fashion Boutique would let her know about soon enough. Thank God she still had her uniforms.

Ronnie went through all the revisions stuffed in her mailbox. She only had the rest of this bid period with Flip before she'd be relegated to reserve status again. She still wasn't sure how Flip had managed to get her back on his schedule. She had a sneaky suspicion that he'd done some trip trading to get them booked together for more time than just the original one month. He'd been with the company long enough to have a lot of clout with operations and crew alike. Very persuasive man. Her thoughts drifted to their last bedroom encounter. *Very persuasive, indeed.*

Hopefully their flight today would land on schedule and they could ring in the new year at Times Square. Or maybe they'd have a quiet dinner for two in their room.

She thanked her lucky stars not only that she got to work with Flip, but that she'd been spared flying reserve. It'd been heaven to know what days she worked and where she was going. She could almost have a life.

Gathering the stacks of envelopes on the counter, she started for the door, pausing at the company bulletin board to scan any announcements that might be of interest.

On a three-by-five card was an ad for mixed Labrador puppies. The sale amount had been red-penciled twice until the notice now read, *Two left, free to good home.* Ronnie chuckled. The owner sounded desperate. Thinking of Pickles and listening to Ginny's story of the cocker's rampage in her closet was enough to squelch Ronnie's desire for something warm and fuzzy to liven up her condo. Especially when she was headed for reserve status again.

Out of the corner of her eye, she caught a glimpse of company memo. She'd heard rumors that the company was expanding, which meant she'd move up on the seniority list.

She read the memo twice. The rumors had been correct. This was an official announcement that they were accepting bids for captains and first officers for ten new aircraft, the first three of which would be delivered within the month. This wasn't just a chance to get off reserve; they were accepting upgrade bids.

At least five or six crews would be needed for each plane, and even if she didn't get an upgrade to a different aircraft, those who did would give her a chance to get off of reserve altogether.

The normal upgrade process usually took a long path, but these were not normal times. With deregulation, the airline industry had changed. Competition was fierce and being the biggest and most efficient was the name of the game. A lot of smaller airlines had bit the dust and things didn't look too rosy for some of the large carriers, either. Global was making noises about merging and there'd even been talk of a hostile takeover of their closest rival.

She wondered if Flip would opt for upgrading to a different aircraft. Of course, there would be days of boring ground school and hours of simulator training along with all the nail-biting tension that comes with proving you can do the job to the FAA and the company. She had no doubt he'd breeze through it.

Ronnie jotted down the deadline to submit bids and figured, at the least, she'd end up holding a line as first officer. Maybe she and Flip could get blocked together again. Scrambling through her flight bag, Ronnie found a bid sheet and quickly filled out the necessary information. She knew approximately where she was on the seniority list and the excitement bubbled up in spite of her efforts to be cool and calm.

Ronnie took the form and walked down the short hallway to the chief pilot's office to deposit it in the bid box on the desk. It was a relief to her that the chief pilot was out. She wasn't sure she wanted anyone to know just yet how brazen a step she was taking. Euphoria that held the scent of success swept over her. She hoped this was one step closer to becoming Captain Talbot. It sounded really good.

Returning to the main area, Ronnie recognized a tall redhead in a group of flight attendants just coming through the main door.

"Hello, Janet. Are you on my flight today?"

Janet scowled. "I can't believe I have to work on New Year's Eve. This is so unfair."

"Yeah, I know, but somebody has to do it." Ronnie tried to sympathize, but in reality, she was thrilled with the idea of spending New Year's Eve with Flip.

"Huh, easy for you to say. If I had your inside connections, I guess I'd be a good sport about it too."

"What is that supposed to mean?" Janet had never been friendly to her, but Ronnie always tried her best to be civil.

"Oh, come on. You can't be that naive." Janet looked around the room and then moved closer so only Ronnie could hear. "Everyone knows Flip bribed all the schedulers in order to have the exclusive track with you. Tell me, Talbot: Does Flip still make smooth landings every time?"

The blood drained from her face. Ronnie suddenly felt like she was back on that pageant stage seven years ago. Back then it was the runner-up in the Miss Citrus of Dade County competition who had hurled the accusations. Ronnie had denied and protested; then she'd found out the truth. Her talent and poise on the stage did not win some of the pageants. The specialty "work" her mother had performed with the judges the night before was what had placed the crown on Ronnie's head.

"I don't know what you're talking about." Ronnie's voice didn't sound as indignant as she'd hoped.

"Flip boasted he could melt the ice princess, and with help from his buddies in scheduling, I'd say he did a pretty good job. Why, now she's even friendly with little old insignificant me."

Green, cat-like eyes bore into Ronnie like hot pokers, and in that moment, Ronnie knew there was truth to the ugly words.

Janet's image blurred as Ronnie bolted past her and rushed from the room. Heart pounding louder than her heels on the marble floor, Ronnie ran through the terminal. Seeing the stick figure indicating the ladies room, she veered sharply, almost colliding with an elderly lady.

"My goodness, you must be in a hurry. Good luck." The woman flattened herself against the wall as Ronnie dove for one of the cubicles and slammed the door.

Leaning her head against the cool metal partition, Ronnie willed her heart to slow its pace. Had she really been such an easy mark? Up to now, she'd never taken anything for granted. After the things her mother had pulled, Ronnie had trained herself to question and be skeptical. She should have known getting blocked with Flip was too good to be true. All that talk about her being a good pilot—he only said it to get her in bed.

But what was she going to do about it? Glancing at her watch, she saw there wasn't much time before she'd have to face him.

~~~

Flip came on board the aircraft, surprised Ronnie wasn't there ahead of him doing the preflight. God knows she always arrived early enough to preflight the entire Global fleet besides the plane she'd be flying.

The thought of how cute she'd been this morning made him smile. She'd realized her flight manual wasn't current and had panicked. She was so by-the-book. Some pilots procrastinated until the threat of an FAA inspector on board would prompt them to check their manuals for perfection.

He jotted down weight and balance information and communicated with ground control, all the while watching for Ronnie. It wasn't like her to be late.

Although it was the first officer's responsibility, he'd gone ahead and finished the preflight both in and out of the aircraft, instructed the crew and checked the weather twice. He managed it all while trying to avoid getting trapped in the galley with Janet.

From the minute he'd checked in today, the flight attendant had been making none-too-subtle passes at him. Since he and Ronnie hadn't attempted to hide their relationship, he couldn't understand Janet's behavior. He'd said or done nothing toward her that could be even remotely considered encouragement.

Hearing a rustle behind him, Flip turned to see Ronnie hanging her coat in the crew compartment. A silent sigh of relief surged through his body. "Hey, where you been? I was about ready to send out the rescue squad. I did the walk-a-round preflight."

"Thank you. I apologize for being late. I got tied up." Ronnie picked up the weather reports sitting on the console and took her seat. She immediately went about the business of preparing for departure.

Flip had expected more explanation, but Ronnie remained silent. Since takeoff was one of the most crucial times of any flight, he put his curiosity on hold.

It was several minutes after reaching their altitude before Flip tried to bust through Ronnie's wall of silence again. "So, did you break a nail or lose your brain bag or what?"

"None of the above." Ronnie stared straight ahead, preventing Flip from making eye contact unless he got out of his seat. He was reaching out to touch her hand when she finally turned and faced him squarely. Her blue eyes were cold as ice and her words were just as frosty.

"I had some things to do." She returned to staring straight ahead into the vast curved windshield of the 757. "I really don't want to discuss it."

It can't be that serious, Flip thought, and without thinking, he quipped, "Brrrrrr. The ice princess has spoken."

If the gaze she'd given him before was chilly, the level stare she gave now put him in a deep freeze.

Between clenched teeth she ground out, "Captain Farrell, I'm on duty as first officer, and if you try to make it anything but that, I'll file appropriate charges."

Flip's jaw dropped. "What the hell are you talking about?" He struggled with the urge to jerk her into his lap and kiss her until the old Ronnie returned. This wasn't the woman who'd spent the holidays with him and his family, the one he'd made love to just this morning.

At that moment, radio communications informed them of small aircraft traffic. Flip responded, taking the aircraft to the assigned altitude to avoid encounter.

He looked at Ronnie; her face was like a mask. She'd built the wall back around her and for the life of him, he didn't know why. The last few weeks had been great. He'd actually started thinking about settling down. He was ready to risk telling her that he was in love with her, almost did it at Christmastime. Would have too, if there hadn't been so many people around. It'd been hard to find time alone with her.

Instead of the small gold earrings he had given her for Christmas, he was tempted to present her with a diamond ring. Except their relationship hadn't progressed that far yet—he still didn't know how she felt about him. He thought he had a chance, but now he was more confused than ever.

Ronnie's performance was flawless and she spoke only when it pertained to her job. Flip made a few more attempts to break through the wall.

"Did you get a call from Marlena? She's okay, isn't she? I mean she's not coming back is she?"

"No, she's fine. I think Cory actually finds her useful. She loves her new job."

"Did someone insult you or do something to make you angry at the world?"

"I'm not angry at all, Captain. I'm just trying to concentrate on my job."

Finally, Flip's anger and frustration forced him into silence.

~~~

The flight couldn't have been more perfect: They landed on schedule; the passengers were all orderly and friendly as they deboarded. The hotel van driver was on time and polite. The traffic moved along and even the cabbies seemed to be driving like normal people. For New York, on New Year's Eve, it wasn't just surprising—it was a miracle.

Flip should have been enjoying the satisfaction of a well-organized and expertly managed trip. Instead, sitting in the van on the way to the hotel, he was as depressed as if he'd just busted his line check and was destined for more time in ground school.

Flip tried to ignore the flight attendants' chatter as he stole a glance at Ronnie sitting by the window.

"So, Flip, can we count on you?" Janet leaned over his seat.

He caught the scent of her perfume, her warm breath close to his ear. He wouldn't have put it past her to stick her tongue in it or bite his neck. It was almost as if she knew things were sour between him and Ronnie and she was taking full advantage of his confusion.

"Don't plan on me." The last thing he wanted was a wrestling match with the redhead. The way she'd been coming on to him left little doubt what she had in mind.

"You'll miss a really good time," the second flight attendant chimed in. She looked young enough to be just a few months past her senior prom. "We're gonna paint this Big Apple really. Really red. Please come."

"Ronnie, are you chaperoning this group?" He hoped the comment wouldn't insult the young crewmember, but it would almost force Ronnie to speak. If she didn't answer, she'd risk appearing arrogant or superior. She knew better than to offend the cabin crew. Getting along with them made a big difference in how smoothly the flights went.

Ronnie's head jerked. Flip watched her gaze settle first on Janet and then switch to him. "I'm sure the crew is capable of getting along without any help. I have plans of my own."

Well, that was a dead end. Plans of her own? Did she have an old flame in New York? Something had definitely happened between the time she'd left his house this morning and when they'd met again in the aircraft. It was as if the closeness they'd had over the holidays had never existed. As soon as they got to the hotel room, he'd get to the bottom of whatever had returned Ronnie to her frigid former self.

~~~

Ronnie lay down on her bed and tried not to think about Flip in an identical room a few doors down. He'd seemed actually shocked when she hadn't followed him in like always. God knows she'd wanted to. Grabbing the pillow next to her, Ronnie punched it vigorously, then hugged it close to her chest.

"It's back to plan A for me. No more detours."

Closing her eyes, she tried to block out Flip's image. She was no more successful at that than she was at keeping the tears from rolling into her ears.

It'd been so hard to leave his bed this morning. Sleeping, his handsome face took on a little boy quality, and while she'd not been around many children, she knew he'd been an adorable baby.

Remembering his tousled hair and the irresistible cleft in his chin, she'd never even gotten a foot on the floor before she'd smothered his face with kisses. As her lips grazed his eyelids, he'd awakened and they'd made love.

Hammers pounded in her temples as her nagging headache went on max sound. Then she realized the noise was someone knocking at her door. She didn't have to think twice to guess who it was. Not sure she was ready for Flip and yet knowing he'd keep banging on the door until she opened it. She yelled, "All right! I'm coming."

Ronnie threw open the door and he brushed past her and strode to the middle of the room. She shut the door, leaned against it and took a deep breath. Putting on her best cool-and-collected face, and hoping her tears hadn't left telltale streaks, she strolled over to face him, arms crossed.

"Would you care to give me a rational explanation for almost busting my door down?"

She could tell the quietness of her tone agitated him, but it was the only way she knew to keep from losing it. She'd had years of practice keeping her emotions under wrap and she used every bit of strength to do it again.

Flip exploded. Grabbing Ronnie by both shoulders, he pulled her toward him until his face was just inches from hers. "What the hell do you think you're doing? I see you out the door this morning, and by the time the plane takes off, you don't even remember my name."

His hair was damp and she could smell the mint-flavored toothpaste he used. It was all she could do not to melt into his arms and blurt out the things Janet had told her.

But it was too humiliating to say—to admit how stupid she'd been. Besides, she'd had time to think about it and it all fit. No one is assigned a block just out of the blue; everything's based on seniority. It also explained why Jack was upset that he didn't regain his slot with Flip.

No she couldn't talk about this. Not now, not ever. She just had to get Flip out of her room, out of her life.

"Flip, I apologize if I caught you off-guard. I should have warned you. From the beginning, you knew that my goal was to make captain. While that's still a ways off, I feel total concentration on my career is necessary at this point. Global is taking delivery of enough new aircraft within the next three months that will allow me to hold a line. No more reserve status. "

She wiggled out of his grasp and rubbed her upper arms where he'd held her so tightly. "I put in a bid to train on the new equipment today. Ground school starts next week if I get the first class. I can't let anything get in the way, including you."

She allowed herself a quick glance and saw disbelief in Flip's eyes. It was probably the first time any girl had dumped him. He was used to getting what he wanted. Well, he'd had his fun, but she was through being just another one of his conquests.

Running his hands through his hair, swearing as he paced the length of the room, Flip started to speak, then stopped. Ronnie watched his mouth flatten into a fine line. His jaw muscles twitched and when he returned her gaze, his eyes narrowed into slits. Through clenched jaw, his words came out like pieces of flint: pointed, hard and straightforward.

"Fine. I know how important it is to be proficient in more than one type aircraft. I get that. But what does all that have to do with us?"

"Oh, please. You didn't honestly think this relationship or whatever it really is was long-term, did you?" Even as the words were spoken, she could scarcely believe they came from her mouth.

"Actually, I thought we were beginning to build something solid. There were still some things we probably ought to talk about, but I thought we were good together."

As he searched her face, she knew he was looking for any sign that this was just a big joke. He was waiting for her to dissolve into a fit of laughter and then grab him around the neck and plant her lips onto his luscious ones.

She allowed no warmth or softening in her expression. It was plain to see, he thought he'd been played for a fool. Actually, she was the fool. *How many times does it take for me to learn I can't trust* anyone?

He took a deep breath and squared his shoulders. His attitude clearly implied his acceptance and acknowledgement that he'd gotten her message.

Well, she'd gotten one too. *I don't need to be hit by a truck to get his little scheme.* She knew it had been too good to last. It was just another fairy tale like the ones her mother had envisioned for her—a life of lights and stardom.

Without looking at her he brushed past her. "I won't trouble you again."

Ronnie watched as he left the room, closing the door without even the slightest noise.

Standing in place for a several minutes, she felt the trembling begin somewhere deep inside, fighting its way to the surface. A heart-broken sob escaped from her throat and she sank to her knees with her arms wrapped around her shaking body.

~~~

Flip jabbed the phone buttons and waited for someone to answer.

"Hello."

The voice was like warm honey spread over a biscuit just out of the oven. Whether natural or practiced, it had the soothing effect Flip craved. His insides were raw and his heart ached like it'd been split in half. All he wanted was an anesthetic to ease the pain. He wasn't sure if this was the answer, but it was the only thing he knew to do.

"Janet? That offer still hold for me to join the crew in painting New York red tonight?"

"Flip? Of course. We're not quite ready, but come on over for a drink. The rest of the crew will be here in a few."

"Sounds good. I'll be right there."

He let the phone drop back into its cradle and raked his fingers through his hair. "What the hell am I doing?" His hand reached toward the phone again, then stopped.

Ronnie couldn't have made it any clearer. Her only goal in life was to become a captain. She was a quick study; she sure didn't need him teaching her anything.

It still was a mystery to him how she could have seemed so sincere. He wasn't the only one who'd been had. His family fell for her and he'd thought she'd felt comfortable with them. Looks like the entire Farrell family were the fools.

~~~

Flip rolled over in the bed and immediately wished he hadn't. His stomach kept rolling and his head seemed to be floating somewhere around the ceiling. Barely able to squint through his lids, he peeked at the body lying next to him.

Lying was an understatement. The form was more or less sprawled over whatever area he wasn't occupying. Janet lay facedown, scrunched into a pillow. Flip wondered how she could breathe.

He raised himself gingerly up on one elbow, and as the whirling in his head slowed, he pried open his eyes a little wider. From the sliver of sunlight that had found entrance through the drapes, her dimpled bare butt shone like the day she'd been born. Arms outstretched from the smooth ivory back; one wrist dangled off the edge of the bed.

Oh God, what am I doing here? What have I done here?

Flip always made sure he met the required FAA regulation time between having anything to drink and taking out a flight. That didn't mean he always escaped his share of suffering. Before his flight took off, the alcohol would be out of his system, but in the meantime, he would pay for his stupidity.

With his insides doing a good imitation of a washing machine set on heavy-duty agitation, Flip eased out of the bed and gathered up his belongings. Relieved to find his door-entry card still in his pants pocket along with his watch, wallet, keys and small change, Flip zipped up his pants and tiptoed toward the door. Not bothering to put on his shoes, he grabbed them in one hand, draped his jacket and shirt over his arm and opened the door to the hall. If he was lucky, he could get back to his own room without being seen. Hopefully, after he showered and took something for his hangover, he'd have recovered before the flight took off. He could apologize to Janet later.

From the looks of her, she was going to have her own bag of rocks to deal with. At least nothing sexual had happened—it was obvious they'd both been too drunk to do more than pass out. Yet how they got inside her room was a mystery.

~~~

Ronnie opened her door to get the free newspaper the hotel supplied, but nothing on the front page shocked her as much as what she saw next: Flip's broad bare back lumbering down the hall. Stepping back into her room, she peeked around the doorjamb and watched him fumble with his room-access card.

Only after he'd closed his door did she allow herself the luxury of slamming hers, hoping the sound would reverberate loud enough to cause severe pain to the occupant two doors down.

"To think, I actually felt like I was losing something wonderful. Ha!" Ronnie tossed the paper on the bed and plopped down in the chair in front of the mirrored dressing table.

"You've been played for a sucker before, Talbot, but never again. You really ought to send Janet a note of thanks."

Dropping her head into her hands, she wondered how much makeup it was going to take to remove the sadness from her eyes and face. She didn't doubt her skill to make the outer picture perfect, but what could she do about the hidden parts still sobbing?

Chapter 12

Sweat beaded on Ronnie's upper lip. She ignored it and concentrated on landing the plane. With one engine shut down and an altitude warning echoing in her ears, she called for verbal altitude reading. Her fellow pilot responded, not as quickly as she'd have liked, but quick enough for her to make the needed adjustment to the power settings and settle the aircraft simulator onto the runway. The visual display in front of her exhibited a familiar set of lights, then disappeared to black.

"Good job, Talbot. You have excellent skills, good concentration and fine leadership qualities." The check airman was a pilot of the old-school thinking and Ronnie had been terrified that he'd bust her flight check solely on gender.

"Thank you, Captain Kensington. I appreciate that."

"You know, Talbot, Flip told me you were a good pilot, but I wasn't sure if I could believe him. He usually grades on looks, not skills. I must say he was right on both counts."

Ronnie wondered just how many other female pilots Flip had recommended. She was one of the few who'd upgraded to new equipment with minimum simulator time. But the good news was the number of women first officers had grown considerably in the past year and a half.

"It was kind of Captain Farrell to express his opinion, but I prefer to earn my way by my merits and not through compliments."

"Well, you've done that." Kensington jotted a couple of notes down and turned off the power in the simulator. Handing her the small slip of paper, Kensington smiled, "Congratulations, Talbot." He extended his hand and popped the door open.

Relief spread through her as if a five-hundred-pound weight had been lifted from her shoulders. Her check ride in the new equipment had gone well. She'd proved she was a person to be recognized for what she could do, not how she looked wearing a sash over a bathing suit or pink satin evening gown.

"Check with scheduling about getting your line time when the new planes are delivered in a few weeks. We probably won't have any promotions to captain right away, but just keep your nose clean, build your hours, and when the opportunity arises, you'll be ready."

Captain Kensington escorted Ronnie back to operations, where he filed the appropriate paperwork. Casually he remarked, "You're lucky the company ordered the equipment it did. This has made upgrading faster than normal channels. It'd make my job a lot easier if everyone did as well as you. You've flown with one of the best. I'd like to get Flip to instruct for us, but he can't stay out of the sky."

He paused and Ronnie wondered if he expected her to comment. She wasn't about to open up that chapter of her life. It seemed like everywhere she went lately, someone was going on about what a great guy Trenton Maxwell Farrell was. It was getting very old because she knew it was all a lie.

Kensington glanced at her sideways and said, "It may not be any of my business, but have you seen Flip lately? He looks like the wrath of God and word's out that he's a pain in the butt to fly with these days."

"No, I haven't seen him for a while." Ronnie didn't elaborate. But she could have told Kensington that it had been exactly eight weeks, three days, fourteen hours—she looked at her watch—and twenty-three minutes since she'd endured that long flight home from New York as Flip's first officer. So close to him and yet they'd never been farther apart.

He hadn't uttered one sentence directly to her the entire trip back, and upon landing, he'd disappeared as soon as the passengers had de-boarded.

Thankfully, the operations office was just a few paces ahead. Kensington opened the door for Ronnie and followed her inside. After accepting congratulations from the chief pilot and several others, she finally made her escape and headed for home.

The elation she should be feeling after passing her flight check deflated as she thought of Flip. Did he really look bad? Was he sick? Oh God, what if he had some really serious illness? But Kensington said he was flying, so he couldn't be ill. Not physically anyway.

She was right where she wanted to be and should have been shouting from the rooftops, celebrating with someone special or throwing a party. The truth was that there was no one to tell, no one to party with and no one who cared. She was alone.

It was just like any other day. She'd performed perfectly as always. When she'd played the piano, she never missed a note, never flubbed a piece. And after the applause ended, she was always alone.

Now she flew jets just as expertly as she played the piano and neither accomplishment brought the joy she'd thought it would. Her mind went back to the last time she'd felt joyous. It was when she and Flip had made love that last morning together.

He'd made her feel as if she were the most important person in the world. Cherished, desired and, yes, even loved. How could she have been so wrong? How could something so wonderful have been a lie?

~~~

Flip sat on the barstool while his mom put the finishing touches on the salad. He could smell the roast in the oven, and any other time, his mouth would have been watering in anticipation. Now, his appetite was as flat as the beer he held.

Ginny burped the Tupperware lid on the large salad bowl and stowed it in the refrigerator. Wiping her hands on her apron, she joined him at the bar and touched his arm.

"So, do you want to talk about it?"

"If only I knew where to begin. But there is no beginning"—Flip rotated the beer bottle in his hand and met his mother's gaze—"just an ending. Came out of the blue and hit me right between the eyes."

He might as well have been ten years old again. How many times had he come to his mother when he was a kid and she'd always tried to make it all better? Dad had been his hero, but his mother was the one who knew his secrets.

"Nothing happens without a reason, honey. Think about it." Ginny stroked Flip's arm. "You told me that everything was fine until New Year's Eve and then Ronnie became a different person."

"That's right, Mom. It was like night and day. I thought we were on the brink of something really important. For the first time, I thought I had a chance of having what you and Dad have. Now she's back to calling me Captain Farrell if she even allows herself to occupy the same space."

"She's either a very good actress or something or someone made her change." Ginny patted Flip's arm and got up from the barstool. Taking the warm beer out of his hands, she carried it into the kitchen and rinsed it. Looking over the faucet, she said, "I just didn't think Ronnie was into playing a role."

Flip chuckled in spite of his sour mood and grinned at his mother, "No, I think Marlena was the one going for an Oscar in that family. By the way, have you heard from Cory? Is Marlena still hanging with the band?"

"As a matter of fact, I just got a postcard from him. They just closed down Miami, and believe it or not, Marlena is handling all those little pesky chores that come with traveling. She's making Cory's life simpler."

"Well, that's good. The little I got out of Ronnie is her mother only made things complicated and confusing for her."

"Maybe that's where you'll find the answer to why Ronnie is behaving like she is. What do you really know about her, Flip?"

Like always, his mother knew the right questions to ask. She made his brain kick in again. Ronnie told him very little about herself and he'd never pushed for more. She seemed to want to keep it private and he'd let it go. Besides, she'd always pumped him for stories about his life and his family. He'd sort of forgotten she must have had a life as a child, too.

Unhooking his heels from the barstool rung, Flip met his mother's concerned gaze. "Mom, I'm going to take off. Tell Dad I'm sorry I missed him."

Following Flip to the door, Ginny slipped an arm around him. "He'll be disappointed. Are you sure you won't stay and have dinner? You look like you've lost a few pounds. Are you eating right?"

Flip kissed the top of his mother's head and gave her a hug. "I'm fine. Thanks for the beer."

Ginny held him at arm's length and grinned. "You mean the one I poured down the drain? You're welcome."

~~~

Ronnie did her best to avoid Janet, but she knew if she was going to function as a crewmember, she'd have to deal with the flight attendant—if not on this flight, another one down the line. She had to clear the air and work with the entire crew. She didn't have to like them but she had to treat them with respect and fairness.

It didn't help that the captain assigned to this trip was high-minimum pilot, meaning he had to have more available distance between the plane and the ground to be allowed to attempt a landing. Someone like Flip—experienced, talented—had a much lower minimum. Captain Carl Winston also just happened to be Janet's latest conquest.

The captain had come from a military background and was used to calling all the shots. It was obvious he was insulted that he was still required to keep higher minimums in the aircraft than a seasoned pilot. But the ex-military just didn't rack up the same number of landings as a civilian commercial pilot. Being a fighter pilot certainly required special skills, and Ronnie appreciated that. However, when they came with an arrogant know-it-all attitude, she found it hard to tolerate.

Janet had shown up at the aircraft with Carl following at her heels like a lovesick puppy. Never mind the fact that he'd arrived almost on the verge of being tardy. Ronnie had done her job and now wondered if she was going to have to do his, too. She was probably just as qualified, if not more so. She'd heard that Carl was not a strong captain and that most of his talent lay in throwing his weight around. The rumor was, Carl had busted his oral exam once and had barely passed his final check ride, even after the examiner had recommended six more months in the right seat before going for the captain slot.

The minute Carl popped into the flight deck, Ronnie felt his resentment as heavy as the fog she'd encountered during the drive to the airport that morning.

"Good morning, Captain. I have the latest weather reports, ordered the fuel and was just waiting for you to sign off on the charts. I didn't know you were going to be a bit late."

"Yeah, well, fog can be a bitch." He plopped down in his seat and buzzed the cabin. "Hey, could the good-looking FA bring some coffee up here?"

Ronnie knew this wasn't going to be an easy flight. Not only was he neglecting his duties, but Carl Winston was being an arrogant

S.O.B.—treating Ronnie with a total lack of respect, when she'd probably saved his ass by doing part of his job.

The captain usually has last call on how much fuel to order. When Carl hadn't made an appearance and the fuelers were asking how much, Ronnie had made the decision. With the weather looking iffy, she'd added a bit. If they had to circle or divert, she didn't want this bird to run out of fuel.

She didn't know how she could stand to be treated like this before she expressed her opinion. *That cannot happen, Ronnie. He's the captain.* He was the authority and what he said took precedence over any of her opinions.

"Someone ordered coffee?" Marsha poked her round face inside the doorway.

"I meant for Janet to bring it up," Carl whined, but took the Styrofoam cup from the saucy flight attendant.

"Well, Captain, you asked for the good-looking flight attendant. Naturally I assumed you meant me." She winked at Ronnie while Carl turned his back to them and slurped his coffee.

"Ronnie, do you want something? A cup of hot water? Tea?"

"Nothing now, but thanks. Give me about five minutes after we take off. Then a cup of hot water would be great if you find some time."

"For you, I'll make the time."

Ronnie glanced at Carl as he leaned back and propped one foot on the foot bar just below the instrument panel. He put both hands behind his head and actually closed his eyes.

That was the last straw. Ronnie squared her shoulders, picked up the mike and clicked on the link to operations. "Hello, this is FO Talbot on Flight 217 at gate B7. I'm going to need a replacement captain; mine is a no-show."

Carl's eyes flew wide; his head spun toward her as he sat up straight, his foot landing with a thud on the floor. "What the hell are you doing? I'm here."

"Hold on. Let me get back to you on that." Ronnie replaced the mike and turned to Carl. "Are you Captain Winston? Well, you could have fooled me."

His eyes bored into her with a stare that normally would have commanded her attention—she knew she was flirting with disaster—but she couldn't control the fury she felt boiling up inside of her.

"Now, I'm only going to say this once." He lowered his voice to a tone somewhere between controlled rage and pure impudence. "Hopefully once will be enough." He spit out the words, "When you are on *my* airplane, you will watch your mouth and treat me with total respect. This is my goddamn plane and I'll command it as I see fit. You don't put me down like I'm some rookie who just got his wings last week."

Ronnie knew she had overstepped the line, but in reality, he was still a rookie captain and, truth be known, she could fly circles around him any day of the week.

However, she wasn't stupid and she knew she had to do damage control.

"I apologize, Captain. I honestly thought you might be ill. You did close your eyes."

"Then why the fuck were you saying I was a no-show. That's bullshit and you know it."

"Yes, sir. I misspoke and I am sorry."

"If we weren't up against the clock, I'd have you replaced in a heartbeat. Flip Farrell may think you're the icing on the cake, but until you have the four stripes, you take orders from me. You got that?"

At the mention of Flip, Ronnie's heart skipped a jump. She'd give anything to have that left seat occupied by him. Even if he hated her now, at least she'd feel safe knowing he'd be competent.

She answered in the affirmative as Carl grabbed the mike and spoke to operations.

"This is Captain Winston at gate B7. My first officer was in error. Sorry for the mix-up."

She had serious doubts about Captain Winston and wondered who had been the one to finally sign off on his upgrade. The only reason he was in that seat instead of her had to do with seniority. He'd been with Global a long time and just about held the record for being a long-term first officer. He'd said he liked the right seat better because of the scheduling, but everyone knew it was because it took him so long to upgrade.

She was grateful the plane could practically fly itself, thanks to the autopilot, because she wouldn't be able to count on Carl for much. She may have screwed the pooch, but maybe he'd actually step up his performance to at least a mediocre level.

Ronnie handed the flight release form for Carl to sign. "I put on a bit of extra fuel due to unstable weather conditions. Wasn't sure what you'd order but dispatcher was calling for it."

Carl glanced at the form, frowned and hesitated a few seconds. "Yeah, it's probably okay." He scribbled his signature onto the bottom of the form.

Ronnie thought it wouldn't have killed him to mumble a thanks. She'd done him a professional courtesy and she could tell it rankled that she'd had the foresight to think of it.

She put on her headset and addressed Carl, "Shall I notify ground we're ready to push off? Passengers are loaded and cabin door is secured and locked."

Carl grunted and nodded as she made the announcement; then he scanned the switches on the control panel above his head. At least he was acting more like the pilot in command now, rather than some lump sitting with his eyes shut and his feet propped up.

Ronnie leaned forward and peered into radar weather scope. "I hope those thunderclouds have blown through D.C. by the time we get there."

~~~

The thunderclouds didn't accommodate them and even invited lightning bolts to join the party. At one point dancing sparks of electricity skittered across the windshield. Carl almost jumped out of his seat, and while Ronnie was startled, she knew it for what it was. "St. Elmo's fire," she yelled to Carl, whose face resembled Casper the Ghost's.

Flip had told her about St. Elmo's. As the static in their headsets subsided and Ronnie could speak in a normal voice, she said, "It's static electricity. Builds up just before lightening is ready to strike. Hopefully we won't get hit or it could magnetize our compasses."

"I *know* what it is," Carl snarled. "I've seen it a hundred times. It just caught me by surprise." His voice did little to assure Ronnie that he wasn't spooked. She noticed he was holding the yolk with a death grip and his knuckles were as white as his face.

The safety belt sign was on most of the flight with a few brief intervals that had the flight attendants scurrying to serve the in-flight beverages. Very few meals had been requested and the few that were, remained mostly untouched by passengers who were too nervous or queasy to eat.

It had been a long flight and everyone just wanted to land, including Ronnie. Flying with Carl couldn't even compare with the flights she'd had with Flip. She admired Flip's ability and professionalism more now than ever. She remembered how he'd let her make the landing into San Diego on their first trip together. But while she wasn't totally comfortable with Carl at the controls, she couldn't say a word. It was a given that Carl would not give her any landings, even though she was pretty sure she'd be able to do as good a job—or better.

"Captain, we're twenty-five miles out from the airport. Center just gave us restrictions due to outbound aircraft. Set altimeter to twenty-nine point fifty-four. I'll work the radio."

She stole a glance at Carl and wasn't sure if he'd heard her. She repeated the instructions she'd been given, "Set altimeter—"

"I heard you," he snarled.

"Maybe we should ask for a vector around this mess. Or maybe we could land at an alternate."

"No way. I am not putting this bird down anywhere but our destination. I don't want to be up here longer than necessary. We'll have the airport in sight any minute now."

"Yeah, maybe. If we can see anything, that is."

"I don't need your smartass remarks." Then Carl almost yelled, "Get on the horn and tell the passengers they need to stay in their seats. The FAs too. No service. It's going to be rough as crap. I don't like this at all." His eyes darted across the windshield and flinched when a bolt of lightning flashed in front of them.

Before Ronnie had finished making the cabin announcement, Carl barked another order. "Also get ahold of company and see if we've got an assigned gate. I don't want to be circling around in this mess while they get their head out of their ass to give us landing instructions."

"Can you let me know when you reach twelve thousand, then hold until I get further clearance."

"Of course." Carl's voice was raspy, and Ronnie couldn't help but notice a sheen of perspiration on his upper lip. Ronnie wished she were in command. Keeping her eyes on the instruments and her ears tuned to the air traffic control instructions, she glanced at Carl and saw that he'd not relaxed a bit. Boy, this was going to be interesting.

She looked out the windshield and tried to assess the cloud cover as they were closing in at twenty miles out. Ronnie finished jotting down the information she was getting from traffic control. Before she could contact Global operations, the resolution alert went off, sending shock waves through Ronnie's body. Her senses went on full alert.

"Traffic. Traffic. Climb." The Traffic Collision Avoidance System went into action, instructing the aircraft to ascend immediately to twelve thousand. Center crackled through the radio. "State altitude. I told you 12,000. You're low. Traffic at three o'clock. Pull up immediately."

She stole a quick glance at the man in the left seat, frozen at the controls. "Altitude. Altitude. *Climb,* Carl!" Not waiting for his response, she almost screamed at him, "I got it, Carl."

She grabbed the yolk and applied power, and the huge aircraft climbed from its descent. Her heart pounded almost as fast as she'd geared up the plane to travel. She scanned the sky as the nose of the plane rose above the dark clouds, revealing a small corporate jet passing under them by about two miles.

"Center, this is Global 217, we noted your traffic and have now climbed to one two thousand."

"Roger, Global 217, I'm going to hand you over to approach now."

"Copy that. Thank you."

It was a check ride all over again, but this time it was for real. She couldn't make any mistakes and expect a second chance.

Glancing quickly, she saw nothing else in their lane, then checked the altimeter before exhaling. She hadn't realized she'd been holding her breath. She checked the instruments and determined almost immediately what had gone awry.

Evidently, Carl had set the altimeter to the wrong atmospheric pressure reading and this had resulted in a misreading of actual altitude. They'd been below 12,000 and too close to the lane in which the small jet had been traveling.

Ronnie communicated with the tower and stepped the altitude down as the airport came into sight. The weather had not softened into a gentle rainfall as Ronnie had hoped would happen once they got closer to the airport, but continued to pour along with the drama of lightning bolts and thunder roars.

Gulping a bite of air, she wet her lips and then spoke as calmly as she could. "Carl, did you reset the altimeter when I gave the reading?"

"Of course. Did you set yours?"

"I think so. I was going to and then you told me to make cabin announcement."

At that moment, the plane shook and another flash of lightning struck close by. Streams of rain hit the windshield, making it almost impossible for the wipers to maintain any visuals.

Carl made no attempt to take over. He sat almost frozen in place. The sweat rolled down his face unchecked, dampening his sideburns and shirt collar.

Ronnie received final instructions. Fortunately, the final descent was uneventful, and after what seemed like hours, the tires finally bumped and rolled onto the runway. Ronnie taxied into position and toward their assigned gate.

Only then did Carl seem to rejoin the living. In an almost adequate, if still a tad shaky, voice, Carl spoke, "FO Talbot, I'll make the final cabin announcement."

She wondered if he could manage that much. His face was pale and a mist of sweat still covered his forehead and upper lip. *Why is he sweating? I did all the labor.*

Come to think of it, the back of her neck was damp and her throat felt like she swallowed a handful of sand. There was no more conversation until they had come to a full stop at the gate and Ronnie shut down the power.

Carl pulled off his headset and sat with his hands folded in his lap, staring into space.

Ronnie fought to keep her voice normal. She handed him the logbook and waited until he'd signed it. She closed it and deposited it in the proper place.

Several minutes passed. Quietly she asked, "What happened? How in heaven's name could you bust altitude like that?"

Carl looked at her blankly. "I don't know. I thought I was okay." Then he added, "Don't open the door yet."

"I think you might have set the altimeter wrong. One minute you were within limits and then the alert came on."

"That's not possible. I've never done that."

"Carl, this was really bad, especially with the weather conditions and the fact that we were under ATC restrictions. Did you see that small jet?"

"What small jet?"

"The one that came way too close to us. This is not going to be good."

"I know. I'm the captain, but I can't do it all. If that was true, you wouldn't be here. You should have been scanning the skies for traffic instead of worrying about getting our gate assignment."

Ronnie looked at him. "You gave that order." Surely he wasn't trying to blame her for this. She rolled her eyes and let a frustrated sigh escape from her lips.

She glanced at the former military pilot in the left seat again and honestly thought he might break down right there. Surely this wasn't the first time he'd been in a situation like this.

He was so shaken, she almost felt sorry for him. Had he ever flown combat? She was beginning to think not. If he'd reacted then as he did today, he'd probably have been a casualty.

Military jet jockeys didn't rack up the hours like commuter or commercial pilots. The fact that they entered the Armed Forces with a college degree and managed to pass the strict military flight training gave them an advantage when hiring on with airlines. It didn't necessarily make them all strong pilots.

If they were good in fighter jets, they usually stayed until the military took them out of the sky and put them behind a desk as they aged. Carl was too young to have stayed much beyond his obligation. Maybe he hadn't lived up to military standards, either.

Trying her best to keep her tone non-accusatory, she said, "This has to be reported and the FAA will investigate."

"I'm aware of that and I'll handle it. I'll take care of getting the report forms."

Ronnie nodded. "It's better if we do them as soon as possible while it's fresh."

"Of course, I know that," Carl snarled. "Don't talk to anyone about this until we meet with our union reps."

Carl removed himself from his seat, unlocked the door and left the flight deck carrying his jacket and flight bag. Ronnie looked out the window and watched the rain come down heavier again. The dark, angry clouds masked the onset of evening.

Ronnie stayed in her seat. Finally she undid her harness, then checked to see if the Cockpit Voice Recorder was still connected. Not sure if her legs would hold her up, she climbed out of the right seat just as Marsha stuck her head in the doorway. "Hey, you spending the night in here?"

"No, but I'm not sure I have the energy to move."

"Yeah, it's been a nasty flight. I've had my share of hysterical passengers and kids tossing their cookies right and left. Was that turbulence or what? Thank God, everyone was strapped in, but it was a steep jolt."

"Yeah, well, we had a bit of an incident. Marsha, I can't talk about it. You'll hear about it soon enough."

Marsha's face sobered and her brows knitted together. "Oh, wow, I was afraid of something like that. I think we should only fly if the sun is shining."

Ronnie flopped back down in her seat and sighed. "I don't know if the sun is ever going to shine again for me."

Marsha moved over to the jump seat and planted herself into it. "Come on, Ronnie. Shake it off. I admit it was a bad flight, and having *lovesick* Carl in here couldn't have helped."

"That's not the half of it." Ronnie shut her eyes and raked her palms over her face.

Leaning across the console, Marsha touched Ronnie's shoulder. "Well, he and Janet are sucking face somewhere, so why don't you and I find a nice quiet restaurant after we check in at the hotel."

Marsha stood and retrieved Ronnie's jacket from the hanger. "We'll order something really wicked while we vent about this crummy flight, the crummy captain and the jealous Janet of the West."

Ronnie allowed herself to be pushed out the door and wheeled her bag toward the terminal exits. She was so grateful for Marsha's kindness, she could barely restrain from giving the FA a bear hug right then and there.

Ronnie looked on it as a stroke of good luck when she discovered she and Marsha had missed the hotel van. At least she wouldn't have to endure the ride with Carl and Janet. She was completely out of patience.

~~~

It had been the longest week of Ronnie's life waiting for word on her meeting with the union representatives. Now, walking down the hall to the conference room, she wished she could turn back the clock. She fingered the collar of her white blouse and adjusted the lapel of her gray linen jacket. She'd taken extra care choosing attire that gave her an air of professionalism and confidence. Still, her stomach flip-flopped with every step and her heart thumped loudly inside her chest. This whole thing seemed to have escalated out of control. This meeting itself seemed an overkill. What the heck was going on?

While she knew Carl, as captain in command, was responsible for everything that happened on that flight to D.C., she worried about the blemish it could place on *her* career.

She'd had a clean slate until this. It was vital that she have a spotless record—because no matter what the official word was, women pilots were still not welcomed with open arms. They needed to be practically perfect. Until today, she'd never been involved in any kind of incident. *Damn, Carl.*

Because she'd corrected the situation immediately, she hoped the worst she could expect would be a letter of reprimand in her file.

In spite of the fact Carl was a real douche bag, she felt a little sorry for him. He already had such a tarnished record with the company, and this was one more black mark the FAA would look at. Even if she'd been flying the plane, he would still have been held responsible. But she liked to think that if she'd been flying, it wouldn't have happened in the first place.

As she turned the corner, she saw Carl leaving the room where she'd been instructed the meeting would be held. Panic flooded her body. Being late was unacceptable. "Carl, did I miss the meeting?"

"Ah, no…um…they're seeing us separately."

Carl brushed past her and hurried down the hall. She hesitated, not knowing if she should go on inside, knock on the door or wait until she was summoned. Just then a balding man in a dark suit pushed open the door.

"Oh, Officer Talbot, here you are. Please come in."

She nodded at the men inside and took a seat on the opposite side of the long table. She recognized the union rep and the chief pilot. In the center of the conference table was a tray with a pitcher of iced water and several glasses. The balding man, who'd introduced himself as Jay Lloyd, attorney for the Pilots Union, peered at her over his half-glasses. As the other men were introduced, she gave special attention to Mr. Franklyn, the FAA representative. The other two were company officials. She acknowledged them with the same closed expression.

"Now, according to Captain Winston, this was our Flight 217 to Washington, D.C., on March 19 of this year."

"Yes, that's right." Ronnie nodded, not at all surprised to find her throat dry. She wanted to reach across and fill one of the glasses from the water pitcher, but as nervous as she was, she'd surely spill it. The important thing was to look cool, calm and collected. In reality, she was freaking out and suspicious of everyone in the room—as well as the incompetent captain who'd just left.

"You were at the controls?"

"Yes…no, not at first. I was on the radio and Captain Winston was flying."

Mr. Lloyd's eyebrows rose and the other gentleman, Mr. Franklyn, looked up from the piece of paper he held.

Clearing his throat, Mr. Lloyd said, "Well, there is obviously a misunderstanding because Captain Winston stated that he was reading weather reports and you were handling both the flying and the radio."

"What?" Ronnie searched both their faces for any sign that this was some kind of a sick joke. That it had all been a mistake and the two attorneys were just having fun with her.

Their frowns and grim expressions gave little doubt that they were indeed serious. Mr. Franklyn pushed the paper across the desk to her. She read the first few lines and knew that Carl Winston had hung her out to dry to save his own skin. Even worse, she wasn't sure she knew how to prove him wrong. Even if she'd done what he'd stated, he was still responsible for everything that went on in that airplane. What did he think he'd gain? No telling what he'd said verbally or how he'd painted the picture to favor himself.

God, how many of these officials shared the same opinion about women pilots that Carl did? That might make a difference in how they ruled.

Looking up, Ronnie gazed through a blur of unshed tears. If it took every ounce of strength she had, that's how they would remain—unshed.

Willing her voice to rise above a whisper, Ronnie said, "I have no idea why Captain Winston would not tell the truth, but this report is entirely false."

"Officer Talbot, we have your report also, and we recognize that yours and Captain Winston's are certainly different."

Mr. Lloyd collected Carl's report and put it in his briefcase. Squinting over his granny glasses, he pulled his mouth into an inverted u. The attorney said, "Now the problem is—who is right?" Mr. Franklyn rose from his chair and extended his hand across the desk. "Officer Talbot, you're free to go now."

"But I haven't told you what happened." Ronnie couldn't believe she was being dismissed in this manner.

Mr. Franklyn's expression resembled a smile, but Ronnie thought it was more the look someone gives when they tell you to "have a nice day" right after they mug you.

He kept the same stupid look on his face as he said, "This hearing was just preliminary. We'll be meeting with the assistant chief counsel for the Federal Aviation Administration, additional staff attorneys, as well as Global representatives in ten days. Your union will assign an attorney to represent you."

"Why do I need an attorney? Just listen to me and I'll tell you exactly how it happened."

Her resolve to keep a professional tone went out the window—as did her confidence in Global Airlines to give her a fair shake. She was being railroaded, and even if Carl got punished, everyone would still think she was the one who screwed up. Her career would be over before it barely got off the ground.

Snapping his briefcase shut, Mr. Lloyd added, "The meeting will be to discuss and propose certificate action against you and Captain Winston. I would expect you will hear from your assigned attorney in the next day or two."

The men waited until Ronnie found her legs and rose from her chair. Smiling broadly, Mr. Lloyd escorted her out the door. Then without another word, he closed it, leaving her standing alone.

Chapter 13

Hearing the phone ring, Flip fumbled with his keys. Finally inserting the right one, he opened the door and flung his jacket in the direction of the living room recliner.

"I'm coming; hold your horses." He grabbed the receiver just before his message machine could turn on. His black uniform jacket slid off the chair and fell in a heap.

"Damn. Hello?" Clamping the portable phone under his jaw, he dropped his bag to the hardwood floor and tossed his keys on the small table.

"Well, that's a nice greeting from a pal. This is Marsha."

"Oh, Marsh, I'm sorry. I just got off a four-day trip and my copilot was as dumb as they come."

After loosening his tie, Flip undid the top two buttons on his shirt, then wandered into the living room and flopped into the leather recliner. "Ronnie spoiled me. She was quick—I never had to explain anything more than once."

"Actually, Ronnie's the reason I'm calling."

"Is she okay?" His nerves tingled, and not being able to sit still, Flip left the chair and wandered into the kitchen.

Peering into the refrigerator, he shut it without taking anything. He knew he should go through and remove all the blue food. Ronnie had actually gotten him on a healthy food plan, but after she'd left, he'd slipped back into beer and pizza as his mainstays.

"I've been out of the loop on company gossip for a while."

His diet wasn't the only thing that had been altered with Ronnie's departure. Flip had stopped hanging out with Jack or anyone else. He'd become something of a recluse. Being in the house alone wasn't any better though. It was like he wasn't comfortable in his own home anymore.

"Flip, she's in so much trouble. I'm really afraid for her. It happened a couple of weeks ago when we had this trip together. Carl Winston was her captain."

"Oh God, not Winston. What kind of trouble, Marsha? Did that creep come on to her or what?"

His heart skipped a beat and his forehead furrowed with concern quickly replacing the fatigue and frustration. Of all the jerks Ronnie could have been assigned to fly with, Winston was definitely at the top of the list.

"No, Flip, nothing like that. Janet's got Carl wrapped tightly around her pinky. No, it's worse."

"I really can't imagine him being a problem for her—she's handles most things without a hitch."

"Flip, Winston busted altitude and they had a near-miss."

"She made out a report right away, didn't she? They both would have had to."

"Of course, and they already had a preliminary hearing with attorneys and the FAA. Carl blamed it all on Ronnie. He lied through his teeth."

God, what an ass.

"Well, no matter who was flying, he was pilot in command and has to take full responsibility. Wasn't anyone watching out for other aircraft?"

"Ronnie said he was shouting orders at her one after the other. Plus, it was the night of that God-awful storm. I had people puking their guts out on that flight."

"She should be able to clear herself with the recordings in the cockpit, can't she?"

"That's just it, it happened on the last thirty minutes into D.C., and of course we took the same plane out the next day."

Flip's brows knitted into a frown and he pinched the bridge of his nose with his thumb and forefinger. Exhaling heavily, he said, "And the recorder erased the previous day's conversations and taped only those of the current day."

"Right." Marsha sounded as despondent as he felt.

Going weeks without seeing or talking to Ronnie had been hell, but he'd never worried that her job would cause her any problems. Her almost flawless check ride was common knowledge. Her strongest traits were ambition, confidence and perfection. How could a wimp like Winston bring her down?

"Thanks for letting me know, Marsha. I don't know if Ronnie will take my call, but I'll try to get in touch with her."

"I think she'd welcome hearing from you. You're just what she needs."

"Needs me? Come on, Marsha. She used me to learn the ropes. She had her heart set on the wings, not on a relationship with me."

"Boy, for someone so smart, you sure are dumb. By the way, do you even have a clue as to what went wrong with you two? One minute you're solid as Ken and Barbie, then poof—it's over. Aren't you the least bit suspicious about her sudden change in attitude?"

"What's that supposed to mean? I was about to make a serious decision about us just before she left my house that morning."

Flip jerked his tie off his neck and looped it over the lampshade. "By the time I got to the airport, I was Captain Farrell—just after she'd seen the upgrade bids. Very convenient. She just used me, Marsha."

"Do yourself a favor, Flip, and stop by my house before you call Ronnie. I need to tell you the whole story and I don't want to do it over the phone."

~~~

Flip sat in his parked Jeep in front of Marsha's house, still stunned by what she'd told him. If it was all true, no wonder Ronnie turned back into the glacial goddess.

Leave it to Janet to get her nasty little claws into things.

Thank God Ronnie had decided to confide in Marsha. If she hadn't, he might never have known. Janet certainly wouldn't have told him.

The day after the New Year's Eve drink-a-thon in New York, he'd set things straight with Janet. He hadn't been brutal, but he'd been very direct.

On the few occasions he'd seen Ronnie since, they'd both been civil and polite. He'd congratulated her on upgrading to the new equipment, but she'd refused his offer of lunch or dinner.

Now she was in trouble, and he could almost bet that Janet had some hand in it. Not that Janet made Carl bust altitude. That was Carl's own stupidity. But Flip wouldn't put it past her to have given Carl the idea of blaming Ronnie. That was just her style.

Not Ronnie's though. Surprisingly, Flip was discovering that he liked women who could hold their own with men, women like his mom and Ronnie.

"Uncle Flip, are you going to come back and play some more?" Marsha's five-year-old stood in the yard tossing a ball in the air. Flip realized his delay in leaving had the two little boys renewing their interest.

"Yeah, Fwip. Come pway s'more." The three-year-old with big chocolate eyes grinned from beneath a baseball cap that pushed his ears down until he resembled Disney's Dopey.

"Gotta go, guys, but I'll come back soon. I promise."

Flip waved at both youngsters, put the Jeep in gear and drove off. In the rearview mirror he saw them still waving good-bye, and for reasons he couldn't understand, a lump lodged in his throat. It took two attempts before he could swallow it down.

No wonder the flight attendant was always so anxious to get home. Flip knew Marsha's boys were just regular kids, but at this moment he thought they were amazing.

For a while now, Flip had been aware of a yearning growing deep inside of him. He no longer felt the desire to drink until he was fuzzy. He didn't want to drive too fast or take chances on his motor¬cycle. And he didn't want to have sex with just any woman. He wanted Ronnie.

And for more than just fantastic sex. Flip wanted to wake up on a Sunday morning and roll over and see Ronnie lying next to him. To see her slow smile reposition that beauty mark on her upper lip ever so slightly would be like winning a jackpot. Smelling the scent of whatever that stuff was she used in her hair or on her skin could put him in a trance. And tasting her lips would be a small bite of heaven.

He wanted to bring her a cup of her stupid herbal tea. He wanted to share the comics and argue with her over the editorial page of the Sunday *Tribune*. He wanted to help her make the bed and someday take a walk in the park pushing a stroller with their kid in it.

Now that he knew why she'd dumped him, he could fix it. He could fix that and then together they would fix this mess with the FAA.

Flip's grin broadened and his mood turned light¬hearted. As if on a track, the jeep sped through traffic, and though the scenery turned into white beaches along the bayside with sailboats bobbing in blue waters, Flip ignored it all. All he could visualize was silky blonde hair caught by a breeze, eyes the color of heaven and the face of his ice princess as she melted into his arms.

Suddenly it occurred to him that he didn't have a clue as to Ronnie's schedule. Fishing his cell phone from his pocket, he punched in the speed dial he'd added months before and listened while it dialed Ronnie's number.

After four rings, Flip heard Ronnie's polite message. Her voice was like listening to a melody. He waited until the beep.

"Hi, I know you probably didn't expect to hear from me, but we need to talk. Obviously, you're not at home so I'll try and catch you later."

He turned off his cell and made a U-turn at the next intersection, following the boulevard until it fed into the freeway that would take him to the airport. He'd check in with scheduling to see if Ronnie was on a trip. Hell, he'd catch a flight and go to her if he had to.

Now that he knew why she'd dropped him, he couldn't wait to set it straight. One problem at a time. Together they would fix the job thing. Flip popped in a Cory Davis CD, a freebie. Humming along with it, he tapped his fingers on the steering wheel to the frenzied beat.

~~~

Ronnie contemplated answering the phone, but couldn't bring herself to talk to anyone. It might have been her mother again. Marlena had been calling with wonderful tales of her and Cory's wild and outrageous escapades.

At forty-seven, Marlena was having better luck with love and career than Ronnie could ever hope for. It seemed Cory was not as young as his press releases stated. And miracle of all miracles, Marlena was now officially only seven years older than Ronnie and was making her singing debut on the band's newest album.

While Ronnie was happy things were going so well for her mother, it was a little hard to take when her own career was going down the tubes.

When she'd heard Flip's voice on her machine, she'd almost been tempted out of her fetal position on the sofa to answer it. But she couldn't let him know she was home, not looking like she did. It had taken every bit of effort on her part to shower that morning, but that was as far as she'd gotten.

She'd called in sick, wrapped herself in her big terrycloth robe and planted herself on the sofa, unable to move. She'd caught a glimpse of her face in the bathroom mirror and was shocked at the deep blue circles under her eyes. Sleepless nights were becoming a habit, yet it was easy to spend the afternoons in an almost coma state on the sofa.

How could she face Flip? He still was the same man he'd always been. Sure, Janet had moved on to Carl, but Ronnie wasn't getting in¬volved again. And she didn't want to give Flip the satisfaction of seeing her beaten.

God, how arrogant she'd been to think she could do a man's job and get the same respect. She'd always known what she was up against, but this—this was past anything she could have imagined.

She was a good pilot. Certainly better than Carl. But that really didn't matter when no one believed her.

She'd fought her way into this industry and she'd made the grade. She'd come too far to give up and she'd fight this too. If only she knew how to do that.

Ronnie slumped back into a heap, pulled her knees up to her chest and waited patiently for sleep to come and block out reality.

~~~

Flip strode through the door to operations and was relieved to see Donald on duty. "There's the man with all the answers."

"Oh, please, not you again." Donald held his hands up in a no-contest gesture. "Don't get me wrong, I'm grateful for the Cory Davis eight-by-ten autographed color photo that Kaylie makes us display in our living room, but no more favors."

Flip chuckled at the thought of Cory's picture in tight denims and leather vest gracing Donald's living room. With any luck, Kaylie would find a new idol soon. Of course, then Flip would have to find another way to enlist Donald's help when he needed it.

"Hey, buddy, no big deal. I just wondered if you could tell me what trip Ronnie Talbot's on?"

"Talbot called in sick. Third day in a row. She's going to have to bring in a doctor's slip if it goes on much longer."

"Ronnie's sick? I just called her place and got the answering machine. Has anyone checked on her?"

"Oh right, like I'm the den daddy or something. I know she's in some hot water, but I can't tell you much more than that."

Flip's heart dropped to his gut. The thought crossed his mind that Ronnie might have done something stupid. God knows she prided herself on being perfect, and as far as Flip was concerned, she still was.

"Okay. Thanks, Donald." Flip slapped his palm on the countertop and turned toward the exit, only to run smack into Janet.

"Well, as I live and breathe. Is this an illusion or have I the pleasure of Captain Flip's company…in the flesh?"

Janet ran her fingers down his chest and let her nails slide into his shirt between the button spaces. "Oh yes, he's definitely in the flesh."

Flip pulled her hand out of his shirt and placed it at her side. Actually, this could be a stroke of luck. If he played his cards right, he might get more information from Janet.

"Not the time nor the place, Janet my love." He flashed a grin and she returned him one of hers.

"You name the time and I'll supply the place, Flip."

"I thought you and Carl Winston were together now. I don't play on another man's turf."

"Hmmm, Carl's sweet, but he's so borrrring. Besides, he's got stuff going right now and I've got lots of time."

"Yeah, I heard about that. He and Talbot screwed up big time, eh?"

"Well, like I told the ice princess, the only reason she got as far as she did was because of her connection to you."

Flip checked to see if Donald was tuned into this conversation because what he planned to say to Janet, he really wanted a witness.

"So, Janet, I've wondered just what you said to Ronnie before that New York flight? Not that it really matters since she and I are history now, but you must have blasted her good."

Flip forced himself to give Janet a wide smile and casually moved his hand to her shoulder, giving her a mini massage.

Janet leaned into Flip and smiled. Her eyelids closed halfway and she moaned as he continued to stroke her shoulder and neck.

"I didn't say anything that wasn't true. I just told her you were playing her like you do all the girls. She just wasn't smart enough to figure it out. Serves her right that Carl screwed up and she's gonna hang for it."

Flip fought the urge to tighten his fingers around her slender neck, but said instead, "Don't you think you were just a little hard on her?"

"No harder than you've been on me, Flip. I really miss you. Let's take up where we left off in New York. We can start right now—I'm off duty."

"Janet, I know I'll be seeing you again."

Janet's eyes lit up at what she thought was a compliment. He almost let her snuggle closer to him, but his anger was growing into rage and he wasn't sure if he'd be able to control himself. He gripped her upper arm firmly.

"Ouch, that hurts."

Releasing his hold slightly, Flip continued, "But whenever that is, it will be too soon. Your lies and gossip caused the woman I love to turn away from me, and I compounded it by partying with you on New Year's Eve."

Janet's eyes drilled him like daggers. She wasn't used to being confronted, especially in front of others.

Flip noted Donald leaning across the counter, and while his eyes were riveted on a sheaf of papers in front of him, there was no mistaking where his ears were tuned.

Janet pulled out of Flip's grasp; a full pout and a look that was anything but friendly replaced her smile. Flip continued to press his point, "Let's get this straight. I apologize for passing out in your room that night. It was inexcusable, but thank God nothing happened between us."

Her eyes narrowed. "I could make trouble for you over this, Flip."

"Well, you go right ahead, baby, because it ain't nothing to what I can do to you and your candy ass boyfriend, Carl."

Flip winked at Donald and waved. "See ya round, Donald. Pass along the good word." He knew this encounter would be all over the company gossip mill before the sun went down. Janet would be exposed as the liar she was.

Checking his watch, Flip hoped his exchange with Janet had not taken too much time. He had no idea what state Ronnie might be in, and even a few moments might prove too precious to waste.

He raced out to his Jeep and sped out of the parking lot. This time he wasn't going to phone ahead; he'd break down the door if he had to. If she was inside her condo, she might need him more than ever. More than he'd ever imagined. She'd put up a perfect image, and he'd been too concerned with his own feelings to look for the cracks in her icy veneer.

~~~

Pounding on Ronnie's door, Flip received more than his share of stares from the neighbors.

"Ronnie! Are you in there? Open up. Please," he added so the neighbors wouldn't think he meant Ronnie harm. As it was, he knew he'd created enough interest to keep them gossiping for weeks.

He was ready to apply his shoulder to the door when it opened just a crack. In the dimness, he could make out Ronnie's face, and in the poor lighting, he couldn't tell if she was angry or just confused.

He was only aware of the relief that surged through his body. She was okay. He hadn't really thought she was the type to do anything crazy, but then there was so much he didn't know about her. That was going to change.

"Honey, let me in. We have got to talk."

"Flip, what in the world are you doing here?"

The door opened a bit wider but the chain lock was still in place. "Ronnie, I just saw Janet and—"

"Well, why am I not surprised?" As Ronnie started to shut the door, Flip jammed his hand into the opening.

"Please, just hear me out. I know you're in a mess, but first I want you to know about Janet."

"Spare me the sordid details; I couldn't be less interested in your girlfriends." The crack in the door narrowed.

Flip only hoped Ronnie wouldn't crunch his hand before he convinced her to listen. "Janet isn't and never was my girlfriend." The pressure on his hand lessened. "I know what she said to you, and maybe in the beginning I did make some stupid crack. But, baby, that was before."

"Before what?" Ronnie peered out, allowing Flip to remove his hand.

Massaging his knuckles, Flip met Ronnie's gaze and said, "Anything Janet told you was said before I fell in love. I love you, Ronnie."

"Are you serious?" In her wildest imagination, she had never even dreamed this was possible.

"Of course I'm serious. What kind of a person do you think I really am?"

"I don't know. Janet told me that you had to conquer all the girls and then I saw you leaving her room on New Year's Day. What was I supposed to think?"

"That I'm a stupid ass and that I don't deserve you, but you're willing to give me another chance."

Ronnie slid the chain out of the slot and opened the door wider. Flip didn't wait for any more of an invitation and pushed his way in. His voice cracked, "Will you?"

"I'll give you another chance if you'll give me one, too. Flip, I can be so arrogant and so—so—"

"Prideful?" Flip said.

"Well, I wouldn't call it prideful. I mean I take pride in my work but—"

Flip put his forefinger to her lips. "Ronnie, do you love me?"

Ronnie looked at him, and grabbing his face with both hands, she kissed him deep and long. When she came up for air, she whispered, "With all my heart and soul forever and ever."

He pulled her into his arms and kicked the door shut. For a minute he said nothing but just held her close and inhaled her scent. Burying his lips into the soft hollow of her neck and shoulder, he felt her relax and heard a small sob escape from her lips.

In the next few seconds, he wouldn't have been able to recount what happened to them except that his arms couldn't hold her close enough, his lips couldn't find hers fast enough. The sight of her tangled hair and her glorious face devoid of makeup—well, it was like drinking from a cool stream in the middle of a desert.

Her arms wrapped around his neck, her fingers knotted in his hair, and tears streamed down her face as he kissed her. When he lifted her off the floor, she wrapped her legs around his waist. Cupping her bottom, he carried her down the hallway to her bedroom, pausing just long enough to kick off one shoe and then the other as she fumbled with his shirt buttons.

~~~

Ronnie lay as close to Flip as she could and still allow them breathing space. She surveyed the shadowy room and immediately wanted to open the windows, let in the sunshine and fresh air, but if her clock was right, the sun was probably just about ready to sink into the ocean and the air had probably turned chilly. She snuggled even closer, then raised up on one elbow and touched the tip of her tongue to the cleft in his chin, slowly making a trail to his lips.

His tongue responded with swashbuckling action until the kiss deepened into desire and she demanded he take her again. She'd never been so sexually aggressive, but the passion of each thrust drove out the pain that had kept her a prisoner for days.

Screaming Flip's name, Ronnie demanded more and more of him until she dissolved into sobs that just as quickly turned into a fit of laughter. The depression engulfing her since the incident of Flight 217 lifted, and in its place was total peace.

"Well, I'm glad you find this so funny," Flip panted. "I damn near had cardiac arrest at the end." He rolled off of her, but kept one arm positioned protectively across her body, caressing her with small gentle strokes.

Ronnie burrowed deeper into his arms, then abruptly she sat up. "Flip, you said you knew I was in a mess. What have you heard?"

"Wait a minute; let me recover." He made a fake gasp for air, which made her giggle.

"Maybe we better rethink this if it takes so much out of you."

"No, no, I'm fine." Flip sat up and propped the pillows against the headboard. He pulled Ronnie closer and settled her head onto his chest.

Ronnie didn't think she'd ever known a feeling like the one going on inside of her at this moment. She'd known she had strong feelings for Flip, and she'd felt the passion and the tingling nerves, but this feeling was so different.

It was like all the warmth of the world was at her command and she wanted to wrap Flip inside it and keep him this close forever. She popped her head up so she could look into his gray eyes. He looked so cute when he was serious. His brows knitted and he pursed his lips together as if he were getting ready to give a State of the Union speech. It was all she could do to keep a straight face as he cleared his throat and lowered his voice.

"Okay, I want to make sure you understand where I'm coming from, and then there is the 217 incident—"

"Wait a minute," Ronnie cut in. "I've changed my mind."

Ronnie faced Flip and saw the love in his eyes reflecting back to her. He really did love her. He'd told the truth. From this day forward, no matter what happened, she knew her heart would belong to him forever.

"We can talk later." She covered his lips with hers; then she pushed him down on the bed and straddled him. "I hope you're rested, flyboy, because you're back on duty."

~~~

At three in the morning, Ronnie was wide-awake and nudging over closer to Flip. She poked him in the ribs.

"Okay, I'm ready to have our talk now."

He groaned and scooted to the edge of the bed. She ran her fingers up and down his ribs, tickling and poking him into semiconsciousness.

"Go to sleep, woman. We can talk later."

"Come on, Flip. Talk to me now. Other than being madly in love with me, what else made you come pounding on my door like a crazy man?"

Flip rolled over, and with the streetlight filtering in through the drapes, Ronnie could see a grin spread across his face.

"You mean besides the wild sex?"

Ronnie plummeted him with her pillow and then demanded he sit up and talk. Propping the pillows behind their heads, Flip slipped his arm around her and filled in the details of his conversation with Janet.

After hearing how Janet had sabotaged their relationship and learning that Flip had done nothing but pass out in Janet's room that night, she felt better than she had for weeks.

"You have every right to be mad at me, Flip. I didn't trust you enough to even let you explain."

"That would have been nice, but something tells me that you've not met many men in your life whom you could trust."

Ronnie's chest tightened and her breath quickened. Flip had pierced through the wall of ice she'd built so carefully. Her voice trembling, she forced out the words, "You're right. All my life I've been surrounded by men and yet none of them could be trusted."

Ronnie couldn't look at Flip. If he knew who she was, he'd want nothing more to do with her. Still, it was time to be honest with him.

Twisting the sheet in her hands, she continued, "My father never even stuck around to see me enter the world. I lost count of the "uncles" and stepdads Marlena brought home and then kicked out in the middle of the night when they tried to make a move on me."

Forcing herself to look at Flip, Ronnie was surprised that he didn't looked shocked or disgusted. He only pulled her closer and kissed her temple. She made a decision to tell it all.

"Marlena slept with a lot of judges to insure my win in certain pageants. For a long time I thought I'd won them all on my own, and when I learned the truth, I quit competing. I'm not sure if I hate my mother for not believing I could win or love her for the sacrifices she made. So that's maybe why I don't trust men, or anyone really. I have to rely on just me."

"Not anymore you don't." Flip leaned forward and grasped her just below her shoulders. "Ronnie, you're never going to have to fight any more battles alone. Including this one with the FAA. Give me the name of your attorney; I need to know what's he's doing about getting your record cleared."

"Yes, sir, Captain!" Ronnie scrambled out of bed to get the card her lawyer had given her, oblivious of her naked body until she caught Flip's reflection in the dresser mirror. "You're leering." Looking over her shoulder, Ronnie grinned and said, "I'll just leave the card here, you lecher. If I go near you, we'll spend another day in bed." Taking clean lingerie out of the middle drawer, Ronnie opened the bathroom door. "After I shower and dress, you can take me out for a huge breakfast. I'm starving."

Chapter 14

Flip swiped at the coffee spills on the paper placemat, then crumpled his napkin and tossed it on top of what was left of his omelet. Looking across the Formica table, he watched Ronnie devour a biscuit, then pop the last inch of the link sausage in her mouth. He remembered when she'd called a carton of nonfat yogurt and a cup of herbal tea breakfast.

"What?" Ronnie met his gaze, then looked down at her empty plate. "I know. I'm a pig." Quickly blotting her mouth, she leaned forward. "I can't help it. All that *talking* last night made me hungry."

He grinned and, just for a second, wondered if her voracious appetite had to do with all-night lovemaking or the fact that she probably hadn't eaten much since this mess had started. The more he watched, the surer he was that it'd been a while since she'd eaten anything of substance.

Flip wiped a dot of jam off her chin, then said, "Don't you think going without a decent meal for several days might have something to do with your appetite?" He saw a glimpse of remorse cloud her eyes and didn't wait for her to respond. He didn't want any looking back, only forward to the future. "Come on. We really need to brainstorm for your final hearing."

Flip opened his wallet and laid several bills on the table while Ronnie scooted out of the booth. As they made their way out of the café, the waitress smiled her thanks.

~~~

Flip settled himself on the floor, resting his back against the sofa, his long legs stretched out under the coffee table. Ronnie lay curled on the sofa behind him, her chin resting on Flip's shoulder. When she spoke, her warm breath near his ear made it hard for him to concentrate.

"Flip, the whole thing scares me. I've accepted the fact that my record will be tainted, but God, it makes me so mad that Carl lied."

"I'm not sure I have a lot of faith in your attorney, Ronnie." Flip ran his hand through his hair and reviewed the notes he'd jotted on the Post-its. "He really didn't seem to have a whole lot to say when we called him a few minutes ago."

"I know. I get the feeling he thinks I should shoulder the entire blame." She paused. When Flip didn't respond, she added, "Which I would, of course, if I'd been the captain. But I wouldn't have let anything like that happen."

There it was again. Flip recognized that I-can-take-care-of-myself attitude. He knew the last impression she'd ever want to give was that she would expect anyone to cut her slack. The truth was, the captain had lied, damaged Ronnie's reputation, and the powers-that-be seemed all too willing to believe the lies. Flip suspected Winston would never have attempted it if the FO had been a man.

"Ronnie, I'm calling Dad." Flip tossed his pen on the coffee table and picked up the portable phone.

"Why? He's not a lawyer. Actually, I was hoping your parents wouldn't have to know about this mess. It's embarrassing."

"You have nothing to be ashamed of. My family cares about you. Anyway, Dad might know how to direct us. He flew for thirty years so he's bound to have seen stuff like this before." Flip punched in the familiar number.

Ronnie bit her lower lip, then said, "Do you think he ever had a violation filed against him?"

"Not that I know of. But in the old days, when there was no actual accident or injury, the FAA was more apt to look the other way. Can't be done anymore; the sky's too crowded."

Flip held up one finger for silence, then grinned.

"Hi, how's the most beautiful mom in the whole world?"

"I'm fine, dear, how are you?"

"You don't know who this is, do you?"

"Of course I do. My son."

"Which one?"

"The twin, of course."

Flip couldn't help but be amused. He and Mike had started playing this joke on their mother when they were in college. Even now, Ginny had trouble identifying which twin was on the line.

"Flip"—a masculine voice replaced his mother's—"stop teasing your mother."

Flip became aware of a small pocket of warmth spreading close to his heart. Since retiring, his father had become his mother's protector, shielding her from the boys' pranks. It was hard not to envy the tender, tranquil love they shared.

"Hi, Dad. How'd you know it was me?"

"Because I just got an email from your brother and he's in Brazil. Now behave and I'll give you back to your mom."

"Actually, Dad, it's you I was calling."

Flip explained Ronnie's situation to his father. He tried to keep it just the facts, but somehow he ended by defending her ability and praising her judgment. Come to think of it, this was not unlike what he'd just witnessed between his parents.

"Has Ronnie's attorney ordered the tapes from D.C.? They don't keep them but two or three weeks, but if anything was said that could help her, it will be on those tapes."

"You're right, Dad. I'd forgotten about those." Flip's voice couldn't conceal his excitement. His father had pulled the bunny out of the hat again.

Ronnie tugged on Flip's arm. "What?" she hissed. "What did you forget?"

Shaking free of Ronnie's grasp, Flip said, "I'll get in touch with her attorney and have him order them."

A big grin covered Flip's face. "Well, they wouldn't be so critical to her case if Winston hadn't lied and made her appear so inept. He's busted his check ride before, so he's bound to be vindictive as well as jealous."

Flip thanked his father and ended the call.

"What are you talking about?" Ronnie asked.

"Besides the flight deck tapes, which we know are useless since they only keep the final thirty minutes, who else tapes flight crew conversations?"

Ronnie's face went blank for a minute. Then her expression suddenly changed. "The tower," she said. "D.C. National has tapes of flight deck transmissions."

"Bingo! But we've got to hurry. Dad said they only keep them for two or three weeks." Flip keyed in the attorney's phone number, drumming his fingers on the coffee table as he waited to be connected.

"This may not get you totally off the hook, babe, but at least they will know that Carl's a liar and that you weren't trying to be Super Woman." Then Flip winked at her and said, "Even if you are." Leaning over, he adjusted the phone to allow him to capture her mouth with his.

~~~

The hard wooden chair seemed as relentless as the dour facial expressions on the other occupants in the room. Ronnie kept both feet planted on the floor and her hands clasped in her lap. The meeting room was the same one where the initial meeting had been held just over two weeks ago, but there were more people this time. Besides her attorney, there was the assistant chief counsel from the Federal Aviation Agency, two staff attorneys, the chief pilot, director of crew management and Carl and his attorney. This might have been called a hearing, but she felt like she was on trial.

Ronnie gave the appearance of cool confidence, but since the incident, she'd been plagued with doubt. She never dreamed anyone would lie to make her look bad. She shouldn't have been such a smartass to Carl, and maybe should have offered to take the controls when she saw he was nervous in those conditions. She could have used a little more finesse in getting him to let her take over.

Two things in her life had always come easy and felt right: when she sat down at the piano and when she was behind the controls of an airplane. Each one was an instrument of sorts and she'd thought she'd mastered them both. Now she wasn't so sure about flying.

Her only chance of coming out of this with some dignity and, hopefully, her license intact depended on how well her attorney was able to introduce the tapes from D.C. When the tapes had arrived at the attorney's office by overnight mail, she and Flip had listened to them intently. As clear as a bell, she heard her voice yelling altitude warnings at Carl. Then at the end of the tape before the connection was broken: "I got it, Carl." Proof that Carl had been flying—or why would she have spoken those words? From basic training, the pilot who was taking the controls always let the other one know with that short phrase.

~~~

Flip paced the corridor outside the meeting room. He'd traded a trip so he could accompany Ronnie to the hearing. The tape had been just a day away from being destroyed when Ronnie's investigation team requested it. Without it, Ronnie would have had a hard time proving that she wasn't the egomaniac Carl had implied.

Flip glanced at his watch for the umpteenth time. Just the thought of Ronnie in that room with the FAA, union and company bigwigs, not to mention slimy Winston, made his stomach clinch.

Looking down the hall, Flip saw his father closing the distance between them. The easy gait was so like his own, but maybe a little slower. Flip's senses were flooded by unexpected warmth and he took a few minutes to preserve the picture in his memory. He could always count on his dad showing up to give moral support. Even the times when he'd been totally at fault, like the accident in the C140 that had earned him his nickname. As long as he could remember, his dad had always been in his corner. And now Dad was in Ronnie's as well.

"Hey, guy, I was in the neighborhood." Flip stood and took his father's outstretched hand. "Thought you might need some company."

"I appreciate that. I'd give anything to be inside that room, but that isn't going to happen."

Flip motioned to a bench against the paneled wall and both men sat side by side. Almost in unison, resting forearms on knees, they leaned forward. Flip was struck by their similar posture; both of them laced their fingers together and let their chins drop to their chest.

"Dad, look at us. We're more alike than Mike and I."

"Hmmm?" Ken lifted his head and raked his left hand across his jaw. The wide gold band on his finger caught Flip's eye.

"I was just commenting on how alike we are." Flip straightened and leaned against the wall.

He pondered talking to his father about marrying Ronnie. Then, as if the impulse acted on its own accord, Flip blurted, "Dad, I've been thinking of asking Ronnie to marry me."

The M word brought Ken to full attention.

"Really? Well, she's a lovely girl. Your mother will be over the top when she hears. I must say your loyalty during this ordeal surprised me. I thought the two of you had split."

"We did, sort of, but it was more lack of communication than anything."

"That's not a little thing, son. The worst times your mother and I have ever had were because of failed signals. It almost cost me my marriage once." Ken brushed a hand through his gray hair.

The comment peaked Flip's interest. Leaning forward with his shoulder even with his dad's, he began to speak, but just then the door to the conference room opened and whatever Flip had wanted to ask was lost.

Flip and Ken stood as several men in dark suits filed out, each carrying a briefcase, like little corporate soldiers. Winston and his attorney followed them, and it pleased Flip that Winston wouldn't meet his eyes. Was that shame on Winston's face? Flip wondered if the man even had the decency to be ashamed.

Then Ronnie stepped through the door and Flip's pulse quickened at the sight of her. Her blonde hair was pulled away from her face in a neat bun; her makeup was subdued. Fear gripped his heart as he tried to read her expression. He felt his dad's hand on his forearm.

"Ronnie?" He took a step toward her. "Are you okay?"

Ronnie exchanged a few words with her attorney as Flip strained to hear what was said. The lawyer shook Ronnie's hand, turned away and walked briskly down the corridor.

Ronnie looked at Flip, broke into a grin, then flung herself into his arms. "I'm more than okay. I'm flying high."

Flip almost lost his balance as Ronnie wrapped her arms around his neck and lifted her feet off the ground. Catching the spirit as well as the woman he loved, Flip held her firmly and swung her around in a circle. He stopped before he got dizzy and covered her lips with his own.

"Ahem." Ken tapped Flip's back. "Bring Ronnie for dinner tonight. I'll do lobsters." Flip's gaze met his dad's; he nodded and winked. Ronnie eased her hold just enough to wave good-bye to Ken.

Finally, Ronnie wriggled out of his arms and pulled him over to the bench he and his dad had occupied.

"Okay, here's the deal." She grasped both Flip's hands and he thought she had never looked more appealing. She was aglow with excitement. "Because Carl lied on an official report and then the tapes proved it, he's guilty of perjury. It's just like in court."

Flip squeezed her hands. "But what about you? I don't care about Winston."

"All agreed I was not responsible and the overall feeling is that Carl needs remedial training every six months, starting immediately. I was actually complimented on my quick action and I honestly think some opinions regarding women pilots might have changed a bit."

Flip cupped her chin in his hands and tasted her sweetness. He could have gone on longer, but she pulled away.

"Wait a minute—this is the best part. Since my record is spotless… Do you know that I scored higher in ground school than anyone ever has?"

Flip just kept looking at her face and grinning. "Will you marry me?"

"Anyway," Ronnie babbled, "the worst I'll get is a letter of reprimand in my file. After six months, it'll be expunged and my record will be as clean as a whistle and—" Ronnie's voice trailed off into silence; then she whispered, "What? What did you say?"

Flip saw the shock as it spread across her face. Her jaw dropped, and confusion clouded her expression. Flip couldn't resist teasing her. "Honey, that's great. I knew they'd see through that jerk."

"Forget about the hearing!" she screamed. "Did you just ask me to marry you?"

"Well, since you're the only one here, I guess I did."

Like a little girl on Christmas morning, Ronnie's eyes widened and her mouth tilted into a smile that grew until it reached from ear to ear. Voice bubbling with excitement, she jabbered something that sounded like "yes" and threw both arms around Flip's neck.

He inhaled her scent and tasted her lips as her body fit into his arms, so close it was like wearing a pair of custom-made gloves. She was anything but the cool, collected ice princess and Flip couldn't remember when he'd been so happy.

Suddenly, Flip sobered. Pulling Ronnie away from him, he looked directly into her sky blue eyes. "Higher than me?"

"What?" Ronnie looked confused.

"You scored higher than me in ground school?"

"Darling, I scored higher than anybody ever has, including you, flyboy."

"Well, how is that possible?" Flip teased. "I know flying with me gave you an edge, but face it, sweetheart, you're still a girl."

Though he expected something, Flip wasn't totally prepared for the haymaker Ronnie delivered to his stomach. When he doubled over, her face paled and she babbled apologies as she covered his forehead with kisses.

When he got his breath back, he wheezed, "I was just kidding. I've always known you were the brightest as well as the most beautiful pilot in the world."

After he'd convinced Ronnie she hadn't mortally wounded him, she wrapped her arms around him. He pulled her close and they started for the exit. She looked up at him and grinned impishly. "Pretty good punch for a girl, huh?"

They took the elevator down to the ground floor and it took all of Flip's willpower not to stop the car and make mad, passionate love to Ronnie right there, but it would probably have shocked the other passengers on board.

Ronnie was giggling almost uncontrollably by the time they reached the exit. Flip squeezed her hand as he opened the large glass door and they stepped outside. "Well, I'll be damned. Look at that."

Ronnie raised her gaze to the sky. While the offshore fog had started to filter in, the sun struggled to keep pace, spreading a shower of pink and pale orange swashes of color across the horizon.

"Flip, the sky's pink. It's really pink!"

"You can say that again." Laughing, he clutched her closer to him and they headed in the direction of the parking garage. Before he lost sight of the sky, he looked around just to make sure there were no flying pigs around. Girls just might have a future in the sky after all. The flyboys just needed to move over and give them a little room.

Before they got to the car, Flip stopped and turned Ronnie around to face him. He took her face between his palms and bent his head to kiss her. He gently let his lips touch hers, feeling his heart begin to tap dance. When she opened her lips, he deepened his kiss. He was no longer looking at the sky, but even with his eyes closed, he was seeing all the colors of the rainbow and the most beautiful shade of pink flashing inside his head. He was soaring on the wings of love and it felt so right.

ABOUT THE AUTHOR

Shirley Ann Wilder seemed destined to write stories from the time she could hold a pencil. Being the youngest of six children to a working mother, she often got lost in the crowd and turned to books. Reading was an escape into a world that allowed her to do anything, go anywhere and be anybody. She loved horse stories and read every one of Walter Farley's Black Stallion series. She could almost feel the wind upon her face as she rode that majestic steed on a faraway beach.

Shirley met the love of her life while still in her teens and her own romantic story began. Together she and her pilot husband raised four children, German shepherds and Quarter horses, in that order. After her three sons and daughter were grown, Shirley joined the San Diego Chapter of Romance Writers of America and her dream of writing novels became a reality. In 2012, her first e-book, *Too Many Cooks*, was published and the desire that had been merely embers burst into a forest fire. While her books are not about wild stallions or escapades in foreign lands, she offers the reader a sense of romance and love of family, punched up with a bit of mystery and drama.

Shirley's real-life romance ended with her husband's death to colon cancer six years ago, but he remains her hero, soaring above like the eagle he always wanted to be. Shirley enjoys her family, friends, including many fellow writers, and traveling. Since losing her husband, she has visited South Africa, India, Peru and Israel. Last year she and her eldest granddaughter spent eight days in Greece.

TAKING WING

First Officer Ronnie Talbot knows women aren't really welcome in the cockpit, but that won't stop the former beauty queen from pursuing her captain's wings. She's not about to let anything stand in her way—least of all the arrogant playboy sitting left seat.

"Flip" Farrell has a reputation: He can land any plane—or lady— with perfect ease. But his icy blonde copilot has got him in a tailspin, and it will take all his considerable skill to warm her up. Yet, just as she begins to find room in her heart for more than flying, a jealous ex and a deceitful coworker threaten to ground them. Only flying blind and trusting true love will get Flip and Ronnie back on course.

Did you enjoy this book? Drop us a line and say so! We love to hear from readers, and so do our authors. To connect, visit www.boroughspublishinggroup.com online, send comments directly to info@boroughspublishinggroup.com, or friend us on Facebook and Twitter. And be sure to check back regularly for contests and new releases in your favorite subgenres of romance!

Are you an aspiring writer? Check out www.boroughspublishinggroup.com/submit and see if we can help you make your dreams come true.

www.ingramcontent.com/pod-product-compliance
Lightning Source LLC
Chambersburg PA
CBHW070829120626
46556CB00002B/686